NIGHT OF THE
BERSERKERS

A REVERSE HAREM ROMANCE

LEE SAVINO

FREE BOOK

Get a secret Berserker book, Bred by the Berserkers (only to the awesomesauce fans on Lee's email list)
Go here to get started... https://geni.us/BredBerserker

ABOUT THIS BOOK

I have one night to meet the mage...

One night to destroy him...

One night to break the Berserker's curse...

One night to save them...

I woke in a field, surrounded by warriors. The spell had brought me to the threshold of the Corpse King's fortress. When the men seized me, I reached for my power, but none came to my aid.

I was a thousand years from home, a captive of the Corpse King's warriors, and I had no magic.

Night of the Berserkers is a **stand alone reverse harem romance** starring **four huge, dominant warriors and the witch** who must free them from the Berserker curse.

1

YSEULT

The fog stood thick over the moor, heavy as an omnipresent hand pressing down, sucking the air from our lungs. Crows cawed in the skeletons of trees as I passed. The dead grass and disfigured trees were only more proof that the land withered and died under Corpse King's power.

The wind picked up, but I didn't shiver, even though I was cold. Magic hummed through me, warming me even as goosebumps rose on my flesh.

"Every day he grows stronger," one of my younger sisters raised her head. "Even the weather heeds him."

"Shhh," another hushed her, holding a sachet of herbs to her own face. Posies were no use. The stench of the Corpse King penetrated our very bones.

I left them and headed to the women bent around a fire. My older witch sisters stood in a tight circle, chanting as one. The neophytes hung back, allowing the ancient ones to combine power to work the spell.

I remained outside the circle. Silent, though my own lips moved with the chant.

And when shall we all meet again?
In fog or thunder or wasting rain?

When the spell we set is done,
When the battle's lost and won

With the dying of the sun
Moonlight reigns when love doth come...

MY BROW CREASED under the weight of the magic. I labored to breath as the spell took hold, twining around my body like a vine. I swayed a little before I caught the gaze of one of my older sisters.

"Here," the witch beckoned to me. Her body was draped in what once was a purple robe, now rags. She looked like a wasted crone, but when I took her hand, power tingled in my arm. "Are you ready?"

Nodding, I stepped into the circle of witches. Despite the sickly chill, I wore only a thin white shift, with my hair unbound down my back. My arms and feet were bare.

"Child, have you cleansed yourself?" The witch speaking was the oldest of us. I was no girl, but to her, I'd always be a child.

"I have," I answered clearly. "Cleansed with water and hyssop."

"Drank only mead, ate only honey?"

I nodded.

"You're ready, then. You'll walk through fire."

I swallowed and stepped forward. She kept her hand in

mine, guiding me firmly the last few inches before the coals. The fire would cleanse me. Burn away whatever the spell could touch. It was necessary.

It can't hurt me. I reminded myself again as the heat hit my skin. The crone's hand both helped and guided me, but if I bolted, she would hold me fast.

Purifying smoke shot up on either side of me, the heat blasting my face. Tingles spread over me again, as I burned without burning, the spell fire licking but not touching my skin.

Once I made it through, I took a deep breath of cool air. I felt lighter, empty. A vessel for the spell, the great power my sisters and I would call into my being.

"The cleansing is finished. Let the spell begin."

I took my place on the cold rock as my sisters gathered around me. Ancient hands raised, the younger neophytes huddled behind, heads bowed, arms linked for protection.

I steadied my breathing and looked within.

I could do this.

Of all my witch sisters, I was the best choice, blessed with both power and youth. I must succeed. This spell was our last hope.

I don't know how long I stood waiting for the magic to come. A minute, an hour, a day and night?

When it came it was as if it had always been.

The power rose around me, swirling my garments, spreading thickly over my skin like water, burning like fire. If there was any uncleanliness left, the spell would destroy it, and me with it. I opened my eyes and met the crone's gimlet gaze.

I could do this.

The wind picked up, a great howling as the Corpse King battered our defenses. The outer circle of neophytes staggered and steadied. The crones all lowered their arms. The sky above them cleared, the sinister fog gone. The night sky rolled out in front of me like a black carpet studded with bright jewels, hazy around the edges with the gathering dawn. The stars winked and whirled in ageless dance. Hurry, they beckoned. Journey with us, before the dawn.

I breathed deep, and accepted the power, and rose among the stars.

TRISTAN

I rose, sword in hand, swiping it overhead to drive off the cawing ravens. An endless battlefield stretched from where I stood, stinking of death and blood. My warrior brothers lay around me, faces dirty, armor smeared red, weapons clasped in still hands. I walked through the field of the fallen, pausing when a desperate gasping rose from one at my feet. A warrior lay in the mud, his guts spilling from the gaping wound in his stomach. He was dying, choking on his own blood. Wide, pain-filled eyes pleaded with me. My lips moving in a forgotten prayer, I thrust my sword downward and ended his struggle. I stood there for a moment, keeping the crows off him. His face, young and bloodied and framed with light blond hair, was familiar, but try as I might, I could not remember his name.

In my dreams, I marched on, until I could bear the sight of the dead no more. I ran, seeking the dark forest on the edge of the field. I entered a thicket, hacking with my sword as briars tore at my face. When I broke from the bracken, a silvery light beckoned me through the trees. A woman's voice was calling my name.

Tristan, Tristan. The high, sweet tone was so familiar.

The shadows parted, moonlight glimmering off a woodland

pool. A woman turned, white gold hair crackling around her face, and I had an answer to my prayers.

I WOKE HARD, the woman's voice echoing in my head. I kept my eyes closed, trying to conjure her face, but, like the dream, the scene with the woodland pool and still, silvery moonlight, she had slipped away.

Men's voices murmured in the barracks. Someone was telling a story. Lars probably. He finished, and the others laughed.

I sat up, reaching for my weapon and my helm, feeling relief. I was alive, along with many of my warrior brothers. But as I moved from my bunk to join them in breaking our fast, I still smelled the sick scent from my dreams and heard the buzz of flies, feasting on the dead.

The spell ripped and wrenched me. I cried out as it prised me apart. Vision swirled away, the stars dying, my ears filled with the roaring of time, the oncoming dawn.

The blast drove me into blackness.

I woke with sunlight soft on my face. I'd fallen on my back and my body ached. When I turned my head, flowers tickled my cheek. A blue sky overhead, a field full of wildflowers all around. No fog or cursed stench. My witch sisters were gone, along with the fire and barren trees.

The spell had done its work. It had sent me... somewhere. Could this be the place the ancient ones meant to send me?

As I lay, ears straining, I had the feeling I was missing something. As I watched the wind rustle the new growth on the trees, I realized what was wrong. A day like this should be filled with song, but there was only silence. Where were the birds?

Voices murmured nearby. Male voices. Slowly, I sat up.

A castle stood at the far end of the field, its great walls

dwarfing the trees. A few figures moved in the shadows, but they were far enough away to be no threat to me.

My more immediate concern was the two warriors winding their way through the thick grasses. Their weapons clinked as they came closer. A few steps and they would easily see me.

I reached for the raven's form, waiting for the familiar rustle of feathers to prove I'd transformed. I could easily take flight and be out of reach, winging my way to a perch where I could spy on this unfamiliar land. Once I got my bearings, I could see about my mission.

The warrior's murmurs grew clearer, their chain mail rattling a warning.

Come, I reached for my power, whispering the spell.

Nothing.

My fingers groped the ground, clutching frantically as if the earth could rise up and hide me. Still the raven form didn't come. I felt tired, a little dazed, but not so much that I could not work my magic. But when I went within to draw on my magic, I felt nothing.

Numb, heart beating faster, I sat frozen as the warriors came closer.

IVAR

I caught the scent as soon as I stepped out from under the shadow of the king's stronghold. Sweet as a flower, but foreign. My feet started towards it almost immediately, and though I didn't mention why I wanted to cross the field in front of the castle, Lars was in a good mood and it was easy to convince him to fall into step with me.

"Fine day," Lars remarked, using his sword to hack off a few daisy heads. I grunted my agreement, keeping our path in line with the scent while pretending I had no aim.

"You're quiet," my fair headed brother elbowed me.

"I dreamt again last night."

"You're always dreaming."

"This was different," I murmured. The closer we got to the grassy dip before the trees, the stronger it was, and the more my head cleared.

"The woman? You must go down to the village and find a woman."

"I want no woman."

Lars scoffed. "No, just a phantom creature. A fantasy of lonely nights. A good lay will exorcise this foolishness." He glanced at me when I said nothing to defend myself, looking a little guilty. "How many times have you dreamed of her?"

"It is more than a dream."

Lars snorted again and turned to tease me, but stilled, his mouth falling open. He'd caught the same scent.

"Do you—"

"Come," I said, hastening my steps, now that I knew I was not imagining it.

And I saw her. A bare-armed maid. Pale, with white gold hair crackling about her face. She sat haloed by flattened field grass, stared up at me with wide eyes.

"What is here?" Lars strode forward, holding his weapon. I caught his arm before he could attack. The woman didn't even glance at him. She was too busy staring at me.

I felt as if I opened my mouth, her name would appear on my lips. For we had never met, but I'd seen her a thousand times. The maid in the grass was the lady from my dreams.

YSEULT

"What is here?" the warrior barked. It took me a moment to decipher the words. The language cadence was unfamiliar, the words coarse and guttural. Before I could up and flee, a boot pinned my hip.

I tried to roll, and the warrior's growl reverberated through me. I went still as a bird cowering in the grass before a predator.

"Who trespasses?" The fair one bent over me. His rough hands seized my arm, set me on my feet. I called my magic to me, grasping frantically. But where my power once resided, there was emptiness.

"A woman." The bearded warrior's dark eyes pierced through me. I shuddered as if stabbed.

Closing my eyes, I called again for my power and felt... nothing.

"No more than a maid," blunt fingers pushed back my hair. I flinched from them. *Goddess help me.*

Then I felt it. Pulsing, pushing against me, a familiar stench. It was faint, but it came from the fortress. I'd recognize it anywhere. The Corpse King made his home here.

The fair-haired warrior hauled me close, and I bowed my head, letting my hair hang over my face again, hiding from the dark one's gaze. "Come, little captive. The commander will want to question you."

He pulled me forward, and before I stumbled, his companion caught my arm. Together they dragged me towards the great wall and the pulsing evil within. The closer we got, the more my head throbbed.

Goddess help me, I prayed again, and hung my head in the silence.

The spell had worked in its own, awful way. It had delivered me to the Corpse King. I'd woken at the foot of his fortress. His warriors had me in their possession.

But, whether by the spell or the mage's defenses, I'd been stripped of my abilities. I was powerless.

Whatever the next day and night brought, I would face it without my magic.

LARS

The woman was no match for my brother and I, her thin arm frail in my grip. She stumbled, and I tightened my hold, keeping my face grim as we marched towards the castle. Who was this woman that she could sneak up to our liege's gates?

Calm, Lars. Ivar spoke in my mind. *She poses no threat.*

I almost snarled in return. My bosom brother could speak directly to my mind. Part of the fey gift he inherited from his mother. I did not have the same gift.

As the woman slumped in my grasp, her scent rolled over me. I breathed deep, enjoying the heady smell.

Now I knew why Ivar had been acting strangely. He'd scented the woman and waited for me to do the same. I hated when he kept secrets from me.

Apologies, brother. I was not sure what I had scented. I did not mean to offend.

His careful politeness made me want to growl louder. Our captive looked weak, but her familiar face and scent marked her strange. Dangerous, even.

Her scent clears the mind... how is that a danger?

This time I did growl out loud. Something was not right. Magic was afoot.

I stopped, jolting our captive. She bit her lip but didn't cry out.

"Gently." Ivar admonished as I caught the maid's chin.

"Who are you?"

She didn't answer, but her eyes blazed as she glared at me. She was comely, if a bit too thin. Her features were strong. almost too sharp and wild to be beautiful, and yet the wide mouth, the light eyes, the shock of white gold hair tumbling down her back combined to present a comely picture.

"Lars?" Ivar asked quietly, and I realized I'd been staring.

"Who are you? Why have you come?" I felt helpless, staring at her stubborn, silent face. I hated that feeling. She looked so familiar. Where could I have seen her before?

"You will tell me," I shook her, and she bore it silently. Stronger than she looked.

"Brother," Ivar faced me. "What is the matter?"

"Something is not right." My head was clearer than it had been for months. Maybe years. Every day, I woke with a buzzing noise in my head—some days it was so loud I could barely think. It was always there, even on days I could ignore it.

As soon as I'd caught this woman's scent, the noise was gone.

A shout from castle gates told me we'd been spotted. A contingent of guards marched out to meet us, no doubt to investigate our captive.

Lars, listen to me. This morning I heard a man howling in pain. Ivar spoke into my mind. *It woke me. I had to touch my mouth to be sure the sound did not come from my own mouth.*

I pressed my lips together. I knew what he'd meant.

Every moon, more warriors went mad. It was the curse we bore.

This woman... there is something special about her. Ivar stroked his beard.

"That marks her strange," I said gruffly. We both studied our captive, with her wan face and wild blonde hair. Her forehead creased as if in pain, her grey eyes unfocused. Fey. It would be easy to believe her a fairy creature, fallen into another world.

And now at our mercy, Ivar finished my thought. I turned my glare on him. Sometimes I thought he could read my thoughts, as well as sharing his. He raised his hands in defense, and then the group of warriors were upon us.

"Lars, what have you found?" one called Gaul asked.

I turned reluctantly, stepping between him and the woman, shielding her. Part of me wanted to protect her, but my suspicion and hasty actions had delivered her into the hands of the king's guard. If the commander deemed her dangerous, the warriors would tear her apart.

I made my voice light. "A sweet smelling flower. Ivar and I found her growing near our lord's castle."

"She does have the sweetest fragrance," Gaul sniggered. "What is she?"

"A fairy creature." I shrugged, and the warriors laughed.

"Not a creature. A lady," Ivar spoke up and at his voice, the maid whipped her head around.

YSEULT

Avoice cut through the throbbing in my head. A dark bearded man was speaking to me, brown eyes probing mine. I was surrounded by warriors, wearing helmets of beaten metal that glinted dimly in the sun. Rough hands held me fast.

"Answer us," someone growled—the blond one holding me. I was trapped between two warriors, one with long blond hair, the other dark and swarthy, with a close-cropped beard.

"What?" With relief I found I still had a voice.

"What are you doing here?"

I licked my lips. "Please, I mean no harm."

"Make way for the commander," someone cried, and the warriors before me parted for one taller than all of them, wearing a shining helm and a red cloak. All but the men holding me saluted, with the fists to breastplates.

"Look what we've found," a warrior crowed.

"Commander," the bearded man stepped forward, his deep voice almost musical, soothing to me. "Lars and I were on patrol and came across this maid. We have reason to believe she simply got lost and strayed too close to our lord's home. She is not a threat."

"No? Have you questioned her?"

"She seems to have just woken from slumber. She is confused." The swarthy man placed a hand on my shoulder, squeezing gently. Reassurance? Or a warning?

I remained silent, hoping the commander would think me simple.

"I see. I have never heard of a villager venturing so close to the king's castle. Not willingly." The commander peered at me closer. Our eyes met; I felt a jolt of something. By the way the commander's eyes widened, he felt it too—a rush of power. I reached for it, but it danced away, leaving me shivering as if I'd been stung. I bit my lip to keep from crying out.

"You say she was simply lying in the field?" The mean-looking man at the commander's left asked.

Meanwhile, the commander leaned closer, angling his head as he took in a deep breath. "What is that delicious scent?"

"Commander, if I may—" Ivar started, and stopped when his leader held up a hand.

"Bring her to my tent." The commander turned on his foot to lead the way, and his cloak flared out behind him.

"All right, lass. Now you're in for it," the cruel warrior crowed. He grabbed my arm and pulled me forward, my foot hit a rock and I cried out.

"Have care," their leader ordered, looking back with a frown. Between the slit in the shining helm, brown eyes met mine.

I let the men carry me forward, still reaching desperately for a protection spell. My lost magic was like a limb cut off, one I kept trying to use. How long had it been since I'd felt the flow of power through me, waiting, rising to meet my needs? I felt bare, stripped naked.

The men carried me to a tent on the edge of the field, dwarfed by the stone fortress. More warriors stood in formation, here the grass was trampled, the flowers gone.

"Inside," the leader motioned, and as he stood aside holding the open the tent flap, I knew suddenly what he was. His helmet mimicked those warriors I'd seen ancient murals. Centurions, they called them. Leaders of men. Conquerors.

Either the spell had delivered me to a land where men dressed like warriors of old, or I was a thousand years back in time. My guess was the latter. My gut churned. I would not have to fake weakness now.

The commander crossed his arms over his chest. For a long moment he only studied me. "You may leave us," he said to the three other warriors.

"Sir—"

"Now, Gaul," the commander ordered. "I can overpower one woman."

More salutes, fist to chest, and they left with a flutter of tent fabric.

He didn't look at me, but I felt his curious perusal like a touch, something barbed, sharp on the edge of it. I shuddered.

"Who are you?"

I closed my eyes at his voice. Somehow familiar, it probed deep and set me reeling.

"If you will not answer me, I must find a way to loosen your tongue."

I looked around the tent. An unlit brazier. Armor crafted in a way I'd never seen before. I was no longer in my own country, my own time.

Goddess, had my sisters known what would happen when they wrought the spell? What had they done?

I swayed on my feet. I had to keep my wits about me. I had to survive.

"Sit," the commander indicated a bench.

When I looked up at him, surprised he'd be so courteous, he shrugged. "Cooperate and I'll keep you from harm." He nodded to the seat again, and I sank into it, stunned. He wasn't lying.

"Who are you? Why are you so near the king's castle?"

I cleared my throat. "What king?"

"King Lycaon."

I nodded slowly. I'd heard the name, in the lore my sisters unearthed. It was one of the Corpse King's.

"Are you strange or simple? Those are the only two reasons you'd not know my lord's name."

"Where am I?" I asked.

He removed his helm. Dark hair, dark eyes, a strong face, hollowed cheekbones and a cleft in his chin.

I startled. Somehow, some way. He looked familiar. He was staring at me as if he felt the same. But it was impossible. Whoever this man was, he'd lived and died a millennia before I was born.

"You are lost?"

"I have been traveling," I answered slowly. "I lost my way."

"So you lay down to sleep in a field?"

I didn't answer his mocking question.

"What is your name?"

I hesitated. Names have power. But here, in this place, I had none. "Yseult. And yours?"

He also gave pause, but I sensed for another reason.

"Tristan," he uttered reluctantly, as if the name was foreign. As if he had forgotten.

"And you are commander of the king's army?"

He put his boot on the bench beside me and leaned closer. "Why would a maid concern herself with that?"

"I wish to know the rank of my captor."

"Your captor is the king himself. I act in his stead. I'll ask you once again... what is your purpose here?"

"I promise I mean you no harm."

"That is for me to decide." He rose abruptly. "Guards," he called. Ducking under the tent flap, my blond and swarthy captors came to my side, grasping my arms. Tristan stalked out of the tent. "Bring her with me."

"Commander," the swarthy one began.

"Yes?" The commander's gaze snapped to his man, even at the periphery I felt the weight of his gaze. This one had power.

The swarthy warrior held up under the heavy displeasure. "Where will you bring her?"

"She has trespassed on our lord's land. She may be a spy." The commander paused. "Do you defend her, Ivar?"

The blond warrior on the side of me frowned at his companion.

Ivar weighed his words a moment, then said. "No."

"Then come." The commander's cloak swirled as he stalked ahead.

8

TRISTAN

Sunlight hit the woman's hair, turning it to white flame. The light flickered around her face, the pale eyes, sharp nose and wide mouth taunting me. Recognition danced out of reach. At first, I pushed it, but when she opened her mouth and spoke—I heard the voice that haunted me at night, echoing from my dreams.

Tristan. Every night, she called to me. Without her, I'd have forgotten my name long ago.

Sometimes, I wondered if it'd be easier to forget. It was dangerous to hope. It was dangerous to feel.

"Commander," Ivar was at my elbow, speaking softly. I met my half-brother's serious eyes. Under his beard, his mouth turned down with worry. "Have care. This one is more than she seems."

"I know. I will uncover all her secrets."

"Have care," Ivar repeated. "Some things are best left unseen."

I considered this. Ivar's mother had the gift of far-seeing. I often wondered how much of that gift she passed on to her son. "Do you know something about her?"

He shifted his weight from one foot to the other. "She is... familiar."

"She is to me, too," I answered before considering my words. I did not want to share the elements of my dream with anyone, even Ivar who of all the warriors I led might best understand. "That is strange, is it not?"

"But," Ivar looked away as he struggled to defend the maid. "That signifies nothing. Perhaps I have seen her in a village. An ordinary maid. We should let her go."

"Nothing about her is ordinary."

Ivar's shoulders slumped. He knew it to be true.

"She came almost to the gates of our lord's castle without being caught. There is something fey in her scent." Not fey—beautiful. But after many days bowed under the stench of dark magic, a clean, fresh scent was suspicious. The one that brought such relief must be powerful indeed. "I cannot just let her go."

After a long, searching look, Ivar nodded. I motioned to the men to string our captive up and readied myself to interrogate the maid who was more than she seemed. If I did so loudly enough, perhaps Gaul would be placated. Perhaps I could then let her go, without danger of him reporting her presence. Even now he paced in the shadow of the castle wall, his face lit with cruel excitement as Lars and Ivar led the woman to the whipping post to be strung up. One of the watching warriors brandished a whip and snapped it. The crack made her flinch, but she made no sound. Gaul smiled.

I motioned for the watching warriors to leave and took their place. My own whip was coiled at my belt. I did not want to use it, but I would if I must. Better to make a show of questioning her. Better for my lash to drive her to answer than another's. Better she bore the brunt of my scrutiny than the king's.

9

YSEULT

At the foot of the great wall, there was a scaffold set up with a single rope hanging from it. The blond warrior held me while his companion looped the thong around my wrists. Once they stepped back and pulled the rope until my arms stretched over head and my toes brushed the ground. I was hung like a side of meat, at the commander's mercy.

Tristan stalked around me, his crimson cloak fluttering behind him. He wore his helmet once more; it made him look cruel and unyielding.

I bit my lip, straining to find a rock or clump of grass to push my foot against, to give relief.

For a few minutes, the guards watched me struggle. Gaul's mouth twisted in a mockery of a smile. "This is the part where you beg," he called.

What would I beg for? My life? I had one purpose. My sisters' spell had dragged me through time. They waited on the other side, but not for my return. I only had to live long enough to send them knowledge on how to defeat the Corpse King.

Grasping a handful of my hair, the commander tugged my head back.

"Please," I whispered. If I had my power, I could lay these men flat in an instant.

"Why did you come?"

"I was sent. I mean you no harm."

"Did you come with a tribute?"

I shook my head.

"Where are your people?"

"We were separated."

"Did they deliver you here for a purpose?"

I couldn't lie. I bit my lip.

My questioner shook me a little by my hair. "Do you mean to harm this fortress?"

I shook my head. Not the fortress, or even the warriors in it. I wasn't even sent to harm the Corpse King, for doing so might unbalance the scales of time. I had one purpose, and one alone: find the spell to stop the mage and bring it back to my own time. I only had to survive long enough to carry the message back to my sisters.

I could not die this morn. Not yet.

The commander let go of my hair to stroke it thoughtfully. I'd lost my braid, but at least the locks were still clean. Mostly. He picked a few strands of dried grass out.

"What sort of people send an innocent girl to spy?" Tristan mused.

"She's telling the truth." Offered the swarthy warrior. Ivar, they called him. He still watched me closely, eyes unblinking as a raven's. I avoided his gaze, lest he see more than I wished. "She hasn't lied yet."

"Perhaps she was part of her people's tribute." The blond warrior offered. "She is a maid. Untouched."

Tristan scoffed and paced away, but the blond drew closer.

"Lars," Ivar said in warning, and though the blond warrior stopped in his tracks, he looked more interested in me by the second. Raising his head, he sniffed the air.

"Have you ever caught such delicate scent? It's intoxicating." Lars ventured closer, a dazed look on his face. My feet scrabbled in the dirt, trying to dance away. Something was happening, something I didn't understand. The blond warrior leaned into me, sucking in lungfuls of air until my hair stirred with his breath.

"Commander," Ivar called, and the red-cloaked leader turned.

"Lars," he barked.

The order snapped Lars out of his trance. Shaking his blond head, the warrior returned to his place.

Tristan turned his attention to me. "Tell us what land you hail from."

"Alba. Beyond the sea," I told him, and all three warriors frowned. The expression looked so similar on all their faces, I wondered if they shared a common ancestor.

"Where is that?"

"Where is here?" I asked.

"You do not know the kingdom of Lycaon?"

I tried to remember the lore my sisters had learned. "Arcadia?"

The warriors exchanged glances.

"I heard King Lycaon hailed from Arcadia before his travels brought him to new lands. New lands he then conquered."

"His kingdom is vast. His power unmatched," Gaul said.

"His warriors are also legendary," I attempted a smile,

but the strain in my arms was too great to make it more than a grimace.

"Loosen the rope," the commander ordered.

Gaul jerked back. "But—"

"Now." The commander's brown eyes studied me from behind his helm. I tried to remain stoic but couldn't stop my sigh of relief as the rope allowed my feet to touch the ground.

"What is your purpose here?"

To find a spell to kill his king. To stop the mage from all he would achieve in my time. Any other answer I gave would be a lie and these warriors would know.

The wind swirled around me as I waited.

With a sigh, the commander pulled something from his belt and held it under my chin. A whip made of braided strands. He used it to tip my head back. "I have no wish to mark such pretty skin."

"I'll do it." Lars offered.

"No," Gaul said. "We know your skill with a whip. You would strike her in a way that gives her no more pain than the passing wind."

"Silence," the commander ordered. Lars winked at me.

Ivar cleared his throat. "Perhaps, commander, you should just let her go." Dissenting murmurs ran through the ranks of guards.

"A possible risk to our lord?" Gaul spoke up.

"She is a maid," Lars retorted.

"She is dangerous. She has trespassed and must be punished." Gaul spun in a circle as he made his announcement. His loud voice drew more warriors. I bowed my head, feeling their bloodlust. They wanted me stripped and flogged, if for no other reason than entertainment.

"Enough," the commander snapped. "Gaul, return to your post."

The commander stepped close, his face close to mine.

"Do you wish to return to your people?"

I nodded.

"Who are you, then? And what is your true purpose?" his breath warmed my skin. "If you answer, I can let you go," he spoke into my ear.

I blinked at him, but there was nothing but honesty in his steady gaze. He truly wanted to let me go.

I licked my lips.

"Commander, if you cannot stomach questioning the prisoner, I will take your place," Gaul said, stalking closer. "The king won't want you going easy on a spy."

Tristan squared off to face him, shaking his head. For a moment I thought they would come to blows.

"Commander," Lars called, breaking the silence. "She should be tested."

Was it my imagination, or did the commander's shoulders sink a little?

"All maids must be tested to see if they are suitable. The king commands it." Murmurs of agreement greeted Lars.

"Very well. Fetch the stone," Tristan ordered. Ivar and Lars saluted and marched back to the tent. Disappointment slithered across Gaul's face. No doubt he wished me bared and whipped before all.

"Return to your post," Tristan ordered him, menace in his voice. Relief poured through me when the troublemaker mock saluted and backed away. I tensed again as Tristan come close.

"You should have spoken. I could've saved you." The commander muttered, eyes bleak. That frightened me more than anything else he'd said.

The two warriors who'd found me returned. Lars carried a box. He opened it and a flash of light escaped. I squinted, unable to look away as Ivar took an object from the box and brought it forward. Tristan motioned for him to come closer.

"Please..." I struggled instinctively as Ivar held up a glowing stone. It was milky white, with something swirling in its depths. When he held it up to my face, a flash burst from it, blinding me. A few warriors cried out.

I shook my head, blinking in the aftermath as Ivar put the stone away. "It reacts to her presence."

The commander's face pinched tight, a shadow passing over his features.

"This one must be brought to the king."

MAGNUS

Buzzing bees filled the air above my head. I swatted at them without opening my eyes and spat to rid my mouth of a disgusting taste. Then retched—it was not a taste, it was a smell, and it was all around. A scent like sludge, covering my skin, seeping into my pores.

I had to get away.

My head throbbed. The sun was a brutal master, high in the sky, beating my face. I raised my hand to shield my eyes and groaned. My body ached.

Where was I? Where were my brothers?

I got to my feet and the buzzing grew louder, more frenzied.

Not bees. Flies.

I stood alone in a field of blood. Half covering my eyes, I took a step and nearly slipped on the red-slicked grass. Then the light lessened, and I was able to see the bodies, fanned out from where I stood.

At first, I thought they might be my brothers, but the faces were too young, the skin smooth with youth, still in death.

This was not a battlefield, but a village green, surrounded by destroyed buildings. Smoke rose from the charred remains. I squinted against the sun, but there were no warriors here, and no one living. No one other than me.

I moved, and something clinked against my foot. My best broadsword. The Ghost-maker, used when I rode to battle in service of the king.

Why was the metal wet with blood? Who had I fought? Who had I slain?

I turned, swaying on the soaked ground.

This was not the scene of battle, but slaughter. There was no enemy here. Only boys too young to fight. Boys turned to bodies. Had I killed them all? I could not remember.

The flies swarmed, the buzzing threatening to drive me mad. If I was not already mad. I had fought until I was unconscious and fallen without cleaning my sword. I was a great warrior. I had tasted the battle lust before.

But I had always faced warriors. Never innocents like the ones fanned out at my feet.

What had happened before this morn? Where was my honor? What had I done?

I sank to my knees under the weight of the fallen.

YSEULT

The commander himself escorted me inside, marching me forward with a strong hand on my arm.

The closer we got to the gates, the more my head throbbed. The pain enveloped me until I struggled to draw breath. Whatever defenses the Corpse King had on his fortress, they were strong enough to crush out any magical threat.

Perhaps it was a boon the journey had stripped me of magic. I'd come to seek a way to stop the mage, and now was being dragged into the heart of his fortress.

At great wooden gates, I was walking more on Tristan's strength than my own. His face was grim as he pulled me past the clusters of warriors. I felt his anger, but his hand on my arm, while strong and inescapable, was gentle.

"Commander," a few greeted him, and he barely grunted an acknowledgment.

"Here," he ripped down a fluttering pennant, tearing it into a cloth and thrusting it towards me. "Keep your head covered,"

I did as he bid and wrapped the cloth over my head and under my chin. I kept my gaze to the ground, but felt every stare of the warriors as we passed.

And then, just as we were to step into the yard, a snarling monster lunged out of the shadows towards me. Sharp teeth flashed in the sunlight, the beast—a man shaped giant, covered in fur. Growling, it swiped at me with hands tipped with vicious claws.

I froze. The air filled with a loud, buzzing sound. I caught a glimpse of the swarm—a million raging flies rising from a field of the dead.

A strong arm yanked me back out of the vision, and away from the raving monster.

Warriors were shouting.

"Take him," Tristan shouted, holding me against him. The guards rushed to obey, swarming the great fighter, who roared in challenge and sent his attackers flying.

"Hold him." Lars and Ivar rushed in, dodging and feinting around the monster until they grabbed its arms. More men rushed in, piercing the giant with their spears. Blades nicked the furred flesh and blood flowed. The mouth was still open, roaring, but the eyes fixed on me.

I cried out as the wild warrior's aura touched mine. Angry magic consumed him from the inside.

Whatever this monster was, it had once been a man.

Lars and Ivar struggled to hold him back he howled and reached for me.

"Send him to the dungeons," Tristan shouted.

Lars and Ivar echoed the order, dragging the beast back into the shadows.

I sagged back, stumbling against Tristan. I found myself in the commander's arms, in a daze.

He pulled me into a low building attached to the fortress wall. The guardroom was full of warriors staring at me.

"Out," Tristan ordered them. Rapping their breastplates in salute, they left.

I'd lost my veil.

"Drink this," I accepted the cup of cold water gratefully. The throbbing in my head had receded, driven out, perhaps by the sudden vision of the warrior-turned-monster. That man had been trapped in a battle vision, unable to break through.

I shuddered, and focused on drinking, centering myself so the room didn't swirl away.

When I looked up Tristan was watching me closely.

"Who was that man?" I asked once I had my voice. "What happened to him?"

Tristan shook his head. "My apologies. My man was not himself. I will keep you safe within these walls."

"You tied me up to question me, and now you apologize for one of your men attacking me?"

"You are now a guest of the king."

I narrowed my eyes but didn't argue. My head was slowly clearing. Something about the encounter with the man changed his mind about me.

"I am happy to accept the king's hospitality," I said, a bit formally. If they followed guesting custom, I was safer inside the walls than hiding as a spy outside of it. "And I will lend aid to any of his house. I can help him."

"No one can help him. Least of all you." He paced, his cloak fluttering. "You must help yourself. Start by telling me who you are and where you hail from."

"Sir, I am but a maid—"

"No. Not if you illuminated the stone."

"What was it?" I blurted before I could stop myself. "The stone."

"You are not from around these parts," Tristan shook his head. "If you were you would know. All women must be presented to the king. If you are pleasing, he may choose to keep you as one of his wives."

I sucked in a breath.

"Yes," he said. "Now you know why I was loathe to test you. If you had spoken sooner, you might have been saved."

I gnawed my lip as Tristan loomed over me.

"You should have shoes," he murmured.

I tucked my bare feet under my now ragged hem. He stepped out a moment, calling to a warrior. When he returned, he sat and fixed me with a stare.

"I know I have seen you before."

"I am sorry, my lord," I rasped. "I have never been here before. You must believe me," I added when he rose.

"I do. For some reason I do." He gave me more water. A knock on the door called him away.

"Here," he said, holding up a pair of boots. "Still too large, but the smallest my man could find."

"I—" I was speechless in the face of his care. "Thank you."

To my surprise, he knelt and wiped my feet before helping put the boots on. This small kindness emboldened me.

"Tell me of the warrior we saw," I said. "What happened to make him mad? Did he just return from battle?"

"We have not had a reason to go to battle for over a hundred years," Tristan said. He sounded tired. "Why do you ask after my warrior? Why do you care?"

"I've seen men like him before. Battle mad. Where I

come from, such warriors are called Berserkers. There is a spell to make them. These men have the strength of ten, or twenty. But their warrior's prowess comes with a cost.

"The madness comes on when a warrior fights. But sometimes it lingers."

"Yes."

"Is that what happened to the warrior today?"

"He has been fighting the madness for a long time."

"The hardest fight is within. I might be able to help him."

"How?"

"I have a little skill in healing."

"Healing the mind?"

"Where I come from, the Berserker warriors find comfort in the touch of a woman."

Tristan raised a brow. "You would touch him?"

I fisted my hands tighter in my gown. "If it would help him, I'd be willing to try."

Rising, the commander shook his head. Again, he paced with his cloak flaring out behind him. "Anything you do will only prolong his suffering."

"Do you mean for him to die?"

Tristan didn't answer.

I stood. "Let me try." I put more force in my voice than I felt.

Tristan shook his head.

"Commander," Lars and Ivar entered. They were a funny pair, one dark, one light, but I felt they stayed together more than not. "The prisoner is secure."

Ivar's gaze flickered to my feet and back up to my face, but then he saluted his commander.

Lars stood staring at me. I felt a brief flash of pain in my head, but it was gone quickly. With a smirk, he looked away to ask his commander. "Still questioning this one?"

Tristan regarded me before answering. "She said she can help the prisoner."

Both Ivar and Lars snapped their gaze to my face and spoke as one. "How?"

"I have some knowledge of the healing arts," I said when Tristan indicated I should answer myself.

Lars scoffed, but Ivar looked thoughtful.

"The disease attacks the mind." The warrior stroked his dark beard. "Is such healing possible?"

I wanted to say that it was not a disease, but the aftereffects of the mage's evil magic, but I dare not speak of that. They'd wonder what a simple long maiden knew of mages or magic.

"Even if you could help the prisoner—"

I interrupted, turning to Tristan. "Is it customary to call your man a prisoner, and not use his name?"

"He is no longer himself," Tristan said.

"He will not return to himself if you treat him as a stranger."

"What do you know of the warrior madness? We have lived with it for many years." Lars declared hotly. "It is better to cut the limb off. Stop the spread of decay."

"He is not a decayed limb. He is our brother," Ivar murmured.

No hope, I heard unspoken. *Years fighting the madness and no hope.*

The warriors all faced each other. Lars had his hand on his weapon.

I sat quietly with my lips pressed together. My heart ached for these men, closer than brothers. The magic that gave them power was like grit in their armor, worrying and worrying until it found a way to drive them mad.

"Very well, lady" Tristan came to a decision. "I will take you to the dungeon. But if you harm him."

"I am an unarmed maiden." I spread my hands. "I may not be able to help him. I only promise to try."

12

LARS

As the commander marched the woman away, Ivar turned to me, frustration written on his face. "Why did you mention the moonstone?"

I shrugged in the face of his anger. "I wanted to save her." In truth, I did not know why I spoke. "She will be presented to the king."

"She will survive," I retorted. Ivar cursed, but I didn't back down. For some reason, I wanted the woman to remain close, and safe.

"He may take her to wed," Ivar reminded me, and then I realized my mistake. Desire curled in my breast, next to pain. I wanted this woman near, bathing me in her scent. I did not want her given to the king.

"I've never felt like this before," I said.

"Nor I. My mother told me of a woman meant to be my mate."

"Your mother?" I raised a brow. Ivar's mother had died at birth.

"In a dream," Ivar explained. "She told me a women

would come with hair like lightning, and she would heal our madness and become our mate."

"Hair like lightning," I mused, thinking of our captive's white blond hair.

"She will be touched by the Goddess. My mother was such a woman. And yours too. They have powers."

"Is this magic then? It feels real."

"It is real. I believe this woman is the one who was foretold."

"But when she meets the king..."

Ivar nodded slowly. "He covets the magic of these women. He will use his powers to ensnare her. And we are sworn to serve him." He muttered the last under his breath.

"It's no use, brother," I told Ivar, the ache in me matching the look on his face. "She is not meant for us."

13

YSEULT

I kept my head high as Tristan led me through the castle. The stone hall was clean and empty of people, except for a few guards in each archway who saluted Tristan as we passed.

My bravery lasted until the commander paused in front of a great iron bound door. He took out a key and unlocked it, pushing it open with a grating creak. The stench hit me— the smell of death and dark magic.

When I hesitated on the dank step, he paused with me.

"You do not have to do this."

"No," I hardened myself. "I want to."

I regretted my words as we descended. The air grew thick and cold, shadows flickering like monsters on the dripping walls.

Tristan kept a hand on my arm. He pressed close, and I felt he would scoop me up in his arms if he could.

The further down the harder it was to breathe.

Two shadows loomed and approached. I gasped and shrank against Tristan, who held me. "The guards," he soothed as the shapes broke free from the deep gloom and became warriors.

"Commander," one murmured. Tristan bent his head to speak to them, but I barely heard over the madness like bees buzzing in my ears.

"This way," Tristan gestured, and I went as if pulled, coming to stand before the giant beast that was the prisoner. He was tall, taller than even the commander, tall as a bear. Though he was in the shape of a man—mostly—he smelled like an animal. His bare chest showed great muscles, tapering to a taut waist and the shape of well-muscled legs under his clothes. His arms bore fur and his hands were monstrous shapes, an animal paw lengthened to some semblance of fingers, tipped with wicked black claws.

Goddess help me. At least his face was a man's. As I moved closer, his chest rose and fell as if he'd run a great distance.

"Lady," Tristan cautioned me, and I stopped before the warrior, gazing on him. Malice ran over his face, then pain, then wary curiosity. The shackles they'd bound him with were too small to hold him. Perhaps they had been the right size when they first chained him up, but now they dug into his flesh. Energy pulsed through him—the violent aura washing over me, making me want to gasp. The beast within struggled to break free.

For a moment I turned my face away, trying to draw breath. When I looked back, the prisoner searched my face as I searched his, human intelligence dawning in his brown eyes.

Hope surged. I stepped closer. "What is your name?"

Tristan started to answer, and I raised a hand to silence him, never taking my eyes off the broken warrior.

The prisoner's lips parted. "I have none," he rasped. His arm twitched in the brutal shackle.

"Water," I motioned to the guards.

"Lady," they hesitated.

"Do as she bids," Tristan ordered.

I waited until they returned, and took the small cup, steeling myself to stand closer to the mad prisoner. He jerked his chains as I came close. I held my breath against the stench. His beard dirty. His body marked with grime, but the smell came from the poison leaching from his spirit.

I held the cup to his lips, praying he would drink. His throat moved, his eyes burning into mine. His face was ravaged, haunted, but the eyes were black pits with the fire of his spirit. I would dream of those eyes, I was sure of it.

"Lady, why have you come?"

"You have a name Your mother gave it to you."

"I-I do not remember her."

"Try," I stepped closer and for a moment the poisoned air and buzzing evil disappeared. The warrior lifted his head, his brow smoothing. I laid a hand on his cheek. Tristan moved beside me and stopped himself. A comforting weight at my back as I swayed closer to the tortured warrior,

"She loved you," I whispered. "She mourns for you even now." The warrior closed his eyes as I touched his brow, like a mother with a babe. "Remember her."

His lips moved, but no sound came out. I shrank back, bracing myself for the evil miasma. But it never came. The spell, for the moment, had lifted.

"Sleep in peace," I murmured, and strode to the stairs.

"Lady," the guards bowed their head as I passed.

I held my body still until I reached the stairs, where I crumpled. Tristan caught me, arms like iron bands lifting me, I let him, melted into his great chest.

He carried me to the floor. Relaxed as the evil magic receded.

"Is this how the mage treats his loyal warriors?" I asked and shook my head sharply. "Never mind. I should not speak—"

Tristan held a cup to my lips. Not water but spirits, burned on the way down.

"He was my best fighter," Tristan said. "I can keep these men in fighting shape, but cannot stop…" He broke off and I let my head lie on his chest. His agony poured through me. I closed my eyes and breathed through it.

A touch on my face stirred me.

Tristan stroked back my hair. "You helped him."

"I do not know. That place…" I shuddered. "He needs more care. But I at least gave him relief."

Tristan studied me until I wanted to ask what he saw.

"Thank you, lady," he said and stepped back, formal again. "Now I will escort you to your rooms."

YSEULT

Tristan offered his arm and I took it, grateful for a strong arm to cling to. He led me from the dungeon, through the cavernous halls, under stone archways guarded by great warriors. Though they saluted Tristan, I felt their eyes follow me, especially when our route took us down a covered walkway overlooking an atrium. Clusters of soldiers below turned as one, fists finding their breasts as they acknowledged their commander. Defenseless, still shaky from my encounter with the cursed warrior, I shrank under their stares. Tristan moved his hand to my back, at once steadying and guiding me with firm pressure until we were past.

"It's all right," he murmured. "They won't hurt you."

I willed myself not to sound shaky as I asked, "How is it they turn to greet us even when we make no noise?"

"They scent you." A touch of humor entered his voice. "They won't hurt you," he repeated as he drew me to another great door, wood crossed with iron. "I won't let them.

Another key, and he threw open the door. In addition to

the lock there was a great bar on the inside. One to keep me in, one to keep all other's out.

The rooms were quiet and cool, faintly scented with mint and lavender. Women's rooms. But I'd seen no women on our walk here, or any other, besides the warriors.

"Does the king keep attendants, other than the guards?"

Tristan pushed the door until it snicked shut.

"The king has no need for human attendants," Tristan said quietly, stalking past me, cloak swirling behind him as he led me forward. The rooms flowed into each other, low ceilings and a few windows open to an inner courtyard. A sanctuary, deep in the heart of the castle.

"You'll be safe here," Tristan told me, and I remembered the bar on the inside of the door. The rooms had furnishings—gilt chairs and finely woven tapestries in blues and greens. Sounds of rushing water filled the air—a fountain, perhaps. The noise highlighted the deep, deep silence.

Everything was clean, there was no dust, but the air stood heavy as if the rooms hadn't been used in a long, long time.

"How long since the mage took a wife?" I asked.

He paused in an archway to the courtyard. "It's been some time."

"And all women who venture near the castle are presented?"

"No, lady. Only those who light the stone."

So now I was a 'lady'.

"What was that stone?"

"The king uses it to discern the worthy. There are certain types of women he... prefers."

"And what sort of woman does he prefer?"

"Women with certain... qualities. They are special."

"Touched by the Goddess," I added. I didn't make it a question.

His eyes widened. "Yes."

With a finger I traced the gilt arm of a chair. "We have a term for such women in my time."

"Your time?"

"My land, I mean," I corrected. "The place where I come from." Damn my loose speech. It wasn't like me to make such mistakes. I must be tired.

I leaned on the chair. "Spaewives, we call them. Women touched by the Goddess who possess natural... abilities." Magic.

"Not witches," Tristan said. Again, it was not a question.

"No. Women with natural magic." Women like me—or who I once was, before the runes and rites burned my natural abilities away, replacing them with the power.

Power I no longer had. "The stone must discern spaewives."

Tristan inclined his head yes. He didn't seem surprised or suspicious that I knew what was happening. More... relieved.

If you answer, I can let you go.

The commander stood studying a tapestry of a trio of young women—nymphs—dancing in a field of white flowers. A happy scene, yet the sharp planes of his face were so grave.

Was it possible he knew the fate of any young woman who took up residence here? Back in my time, my witch sisters had told me. To become the Corpse King, the mage sacrificed his brides. Those he did not sacrifice, his magic destroyed.

These rooms were once filled with women. And they

were empty, but for me. I sucked in a breath. Tristan knew my fate and wished to stop it.

When I approached him boldly, he looked surprised. "May I see it again? The stone?" I prayed my guess was right. Tristan seemed to want to save me, otherwise, I would not dare request.

He hesitated, then reached into his shirt, drew out a small chain. A pale light flashed between us as he raised the necklace—the milky stone hanging from the chain—and dropped it in my hand.

"It is the same stone," he said.

I held it in my hands, waiting for it to flare to life. After a moment, it shimmered awake, not with the same intensity as the larger stone they'd used to test me, but still glowing with an inner light.

Tristan cleared his throat. "My mother called it a moonstone. This was hers, and she gave it to me."

"It's beautiful." I turned it over in my hand, admiring it from all sides. My face warmed in its clement glow.

Tristan hovered over me, his breath stirring my hair. I drew back and handed him the necklace. "Thank you."

He kept his eyes on my face as he pocketed it, and I couldn't read his look.

I licked my lips, suddenly unsettled. I felt so strange—but perhaps I was just tired and feeling the loss of my magic.

"The stone... it only lights in the presence of a spaewife?"

A nod, without him looking away. Heat suffused my body; I almost touched my cheeks and breast to be sure they were not glowing like the stone.

I found my voice. "Do you know how your mother came to possess it?"

"She had it when I was born." He tilted his head. "You told my warrior to remember his mother."

"Yes."

"Why?"

"I-I don't know." The way Tristan looked at me, I wanted to put my hands to my face, and hide. I wasn't used to feeling so powerless, or so moved. "It seemed right."

Tristan looked away then. "Most of my warriors don't remember their mothers. At least, not after a time."

Because the mage dabbled in evil rites. The lingering dark magic corroded their memory, and their joy.

"Your mother—do you remember her?" I asked.

"I do," he said after a pause. "Sometimes." He pulled the moonstone from his pocket again and ran his thumb over it. "Possessing something of her... helps me."

In his hand, the stone did not glow, but emitted a faint humming. I felt its energy then—strong and pulsing. Tristan must to be strong to keep it close. Of course, he must be strong, to rise in the ranks of the king's guard, yet still be able to withstand the madness for so long.

"I am glad you have something of hers," I said.

"And I," he said abruptly, as if coming awake, and pocketed the necklace once more. "The warrior you saw... do you really think his mind can return?"

"I don't know." I swallowed and said a silent prayer for the poor prisoner. "But I had to try."

"Most would let him die." Tristan gazed at me with such intensity, I wished I had the courage to ask what he saw.

"He doesn't deserve it."

"Doesn't he? He's a warrior. He chose his path."

"No," I said, and repeated softer, "No. This madness, he did not choose it. It chose him." If the mage did the rite to turn them into Berserkers, then the blame lay on him. But I could hardly implicate Tristan's lord.

"Some say we warriors were born to it. Our strength in battle is a curse."

"It is possible to be strong, and be good," I offered.

"I hope so, lady." again his gaze swept over me, and I felt he heard more than I had said and saw more than I wished.

"Commander." Ivar and Lars appeared in the archway. Tristan and I darted apart. I touched my face, wondering if the moonstone had affected me as much as I affected it. My heart was beating faster. Ignoring the warrior's, I entered the courtyard and wet my hands in the fountain.

"Lady," Tristan called to me. "I must leave you for a time."

I nodded, and he saluted me with his hand to his breast. His red cloak swirled away, and I stared dumbly, numb but for the beating of my heart.

"Lady." Lars bowed. He had a mocking grin, but it was not unkind. "How do you find your quarters?"

"Well," I said. "They are more than I expected."

"So are you."

I arched a brow, feeling more myself with his jesting.

Ivar cleared his throat. "If you wish privacy, we will stand guard at the door."

I thought again of the bar at the door. "Am I in need of a guard?"

"It is not good for you to be left alone."

"Are there so many dangers lurking in this castle?"

"No. Just us." Lars grinned at me, and I almost smiled back at his playfulness.

"Do you mean to tell me I need defense from you?"

"Not us, lady," Ivar said. "Never us. But some of the others..." He trailed off. His cheek still bore a bruise from where the wild warrior had hit him.

"I understand. I am grateful for your protection."

"As we are grateful for what you have done," Ivar said.

I blew out a breath. "I haven't accomplished anything yet."

"You tried. It is more than anyone has done."

"We are grateful," Lars repeated. "Anything you need, we are yours to command."

"Are you?" I purred, and just like that we were back to jesting. Lars' scruffy face split into his signature grin. Even the high points of Lars' cheek colored red. "Then by all means, stay." I sashayed past them, smiling to myself at the weight of their eyes on my backside. Though they were large men, warriors in their own right, Ivar and Lars seemed younger somehow. I felt lighter in their presence, a girl flirting with two handsome men, one dark, one light.

There was a bowl of fresh figs sitting on a table, along with a pitcher and some cups.

"Is this meant for me?" I asked of the refreshments.

"Yes. We brought it, lady," Lars hovered behind me.

"Thank you."

"You would be wise to only eat or drink what we provide," Ivar said from where he hung back at the door. "There is no intent to poison," he answered my worried look. "It's only... there are no kitchens."

"Does the king not keep a cook?"

"The king is very mighty, but he has no court. At least, not a typical one."

He has no need of human attendants. Tristan had said nothing of inhuman ones. If the king had progressed to using magic to do his everyday bidding, he was very powerful indeed. Too powerful for me to face him, even at the height of my powers.

I may have arrived too late.

"I understand. It seems as though it's been some time since the king had any guests."

"Yes, lady," Ivar sounded relieved I understood. The Corpse King was probably listening to our conversation. If not him, then one of his magical servants. I would follow these warrior's lead and take care of what I said.

My stomach growled. I touched one of the figs, hesitating.

"It is safe," Lars encouraged. "We plucked them earlier, for you."

"Thank you," I murmured. The fig was sweet, the juices cool and refreshing. The warriors watched me hungrily, and again I felt hot, too hot. I put my hand to my belly to steady myself. It had been a long time since I had been noticed in this way by a man. Back in my time, my magic marked me as 'other.' I still seemed strange to these warriors but when they saw me, they saw a maid, and not a witch. Another effect of the spell stripping me of my magic.

My hand fell on the pitcher which was filled not with water, but wine. "Would you like something to drink? There is more than enough."

Both warriors murmured assent, and I poured with undue concentration. Lars took his cup with a smile. Ivar made no move to take his, so I set it down on the low table surrounded by couches.

"So," I leaned against the sturdy wood, "How came you to be in the king's guard?"

"We joined the ranks almost as soon we were weaned from our mothers," Lars snorted and drank his wine.

"What? So young?"

"Lars exaggerates," Ivar spoke up. "But the training starts young."

Lars shrugged at my shock. "We were born to it. It's all we've ever known."

"Are there many in training now?"

"None," Ivar said. "Lars is one of the youngest."

"The youngest but the best," Lars boasted. "Ivar and I are both captains. We form the king's honor guard, along with two others."

"Honor guard? Because you have so much honor?" I teased.

"Aye," Lars grinned and gulped more wine. "We do, lady. And we are better warriors."

"And so modest." I crossed to refill his cup and set the pitcher on a low table between us, seating myself and motioning for him to do the same. When he did, I bit my cheek against laughing. His great size dwarfed the low couch. And he wasn't the largest warrior I'd met in this place.

"It's true, though. We are the best fighters. We run faster, we shoot farther. And when we hunt we always capture our prey."

"Always? No matter the prey?"

Lars leaned forward, the gleam in his eye making me flush. "Always, lady."

"Call me Yseult."

"Lady Yseult."

"Just Yseult. I am no lady."

"You are to us." Lars' smile turned coy. How many women had he seduced with that boyish smirk? His long blond locks spilled around his face, inviting me to stroke them away. For a mad second, I contemplated sitting on the low table before him and doing just that.

"Lars," Ivar said abruptly. "Commander wanted someone to patrol the north wall."

"Then go," Lars said to him, still smiling at me.

With a disapproving clank of armor, Ivar bowed to me and left.

"Forgive my brother. He is not used to speaking to ladies."

"And you are?"

"That is for the ladies to say." He hid his smile behind his cup.

"Well, I am no lady," I smoothed my gown. "But I pronounce you well spoken. You have a skilled tongue."

"You have no idea."

I blushed and cleared my throat. "I do not fault your brother for not being comfortable around me. I am an outsider."

"It's not that. His mother was a farseer. A prophetess. She passed some of her ability to him. It makes him..."

"Somber?"

"Cautious. More wary."

"I can imagine, if I Saw all the things that might be, I would be more serious." I didn't mention that I had a small gift of Sight, or perhaps still did, if my magic ever returned to me. "Imagine Seeing your own life—or death."

"Mmm," Lars hid behind his cup as he drank.

"Does he share his visions with you?"

"Aye." Lars drained his cup and took up Ivar's abandoned one. Once he finished that he said, offhand, "He saw you."

"He did? When?"

"He said he dreamed you. Only," the bright haired warrior's brow creased. "I think I did too. And Tristan. We all did."

I couldn't keep my voice from shaking. "What was it about?"

"Moonlight. And your face."

I rose and walked to the fireplace, leaning against the mantel so my arm blocked my face from view. "Why would you dream of me?" I forced a joking tone. "A simple maid?"

"I don't know. Perhaps that is why Ivar distrusts you. You are more than you claim to be."

Curses. Half a day gone, and I had no progress. Who was I fooling? The witches should have sent another.

A slight rustle told me Lars had moved.

"Lady?" he touched my back. "Are you all right?"

"He's right. I am more than I claim to be." It was a relief to admit it. His touch melted me. "I am in a strange land, without anyone. I have nothing. No protection. That is why I keep secrets."

"I will be your protector, lady."

I caught my breath. "You do not know me."

"I know all I need to know." Hands on my hips, he turned me to him. When I didn't meet his eye, he cupped my chin. For all his friendly, open manner, the blond warrior was as big as the rest of them, with strong fingers rough from holding weapons. his face was smooth, young, unscarred. But his eyes bore a wisdom beyond his years.

"Were you sent here to seduce us?"

I bit my lip and shook my head as much as I could with him holding me fast. "I cannot seduce you. I don't have the art."

Lars' mouth tilted up. "No?"

"Please, I'm telling the truth."

"I know you are, little maid. I can sense whether or not you are lying." He tipped my face up. Up close, he had full lips and eyelashes lush as a girl's. "But you're wrong."

"I-I am?"

"Mmm." He dropped his fingers. I sagged forward a

little, my heart pounding. In that moment, I didn't care if he drew his sword and ran me through. I just wanted to be near him.

"I think you know how to please a man."

Heat bloomed through me, burning my cheeks. I stared at him as his blue eyes blazed suddenly gold.

"You already have seduced half the warriors here." He tugged a lock of my hair with a wry smile.

"Only half?"

He rested his hand on my collarbone. My heart jumped under his palm. "You wish to seduce more?"

"No... I don't want to seduce anyone."

"Too late," he bent his head, his breath mingling with mine. "Too late."

When our lips touched, heat flared through me, a fire burning in my breast. It consumed me, spreading with abandon through my chest and limbs, pooling in the cradle of my hips. Lars' lips were soft and confident. As we kissed, his hand slid around to my back, pressing me closer. His shoulders hunched as if he concentrated on gentleness, his body angled to shield me from the room. I was caught between his large form and the mantel, a cocoon of warmth, the perfect sanctuary for a secret kiss.

Only, it was not so secret.

Nearby, someone cleared their throat. I snapped back in shock and would've hit my head on the mantel if Lars hadn't protected my head with his palm.

I'll be your protector.

Tristan stood in the doorway, holding his helm. His gaze swept over us, taking in the empty cups of wine.

"I need you on the north gate." I couldn't tell from his tone whether he was angry or amused.

Lars nodded. "My lady," He bowed, taking time to kiss

my hand. At the touch of his lips, heat jolted through me again, this time rushing to a bright point between my legs. "'til we meet again."

I stayed by the mantel, heart beating fast, one part of me dizzy from all that had happened, the other part of me soaring.

"So," Tristan strode into the room, his cloak flaring behind him like a banner. "I see you've been making merry."

"Wine, my lord?" I asked, crossing the room to the pitcher. My hand shook a little, but I poured well enough, I thought. Until Tristan's hand closed over my wrist and steadied it.

"You're flushed," he noted. "Perhaps you should not drink anymore."

I hadn't had any wine. I stepped back, pressing on my cheeks. My lips still buzzed with the memory of Lars' kiss.

How long had it been since I flirted with a man? I had no artifice. Had I always been this awkward, clumsy girl? I don't remember who I was before the magic remade me into Yseult, powerful witch who bent the world to her purpose. The spell stripped all that from me. I must make my way anew, awkward or no.

Now Tristan loomed over me, his close presence making me feel giddy all over again. I couldn't deny my pull towards this conquering warrior.

"He kissed you."

"Yes," I couldn't keep a small smile away.

Tristan's face hardened.

"Are you in the habit of kissing strange men?"

"He is not a stranger. He is my protector."

"You've known him but a day."

"Not even that long. But love knows no time."

His breath left so quickly his shoulders sank. His bereft expression hit me like a blow.

"No," I rushed, "I spoke wrong. This is just passing attraction. Your brother likes to have fun."

"You need to take care lady. Your time is not your own."

I knew that. I had to break the spell. But I did not take orders from any man, commander or no. "I will kiss whomever I please." I snapped.

He gripped my arm and pulled me to his chest before I could squawk protest. "Will you?"

He was so close his breath caressed my face. "Will you lady?"

I blinked at him and his perfect lips. Dangerous, dangerous lips.

"I kiss whomever's worthy."

"Worthy?"

"There are few men to tempt me. I have not been tempted," I shook my head, "in a long long time."

"We're honored that you find temptation in our ranks."

"Too much temptation, commander."

For the umpteenth time that day, I was flushed and shaking in the presence of a man. What was wrong with me? Even without magic, I should have better control.

I realized with horror. I was a spaewife. A creature with earthly desires. Goddess made, passion. The fever would overtake me. I had left it behind when I underwent my initiation into the sacred arts. The power I handled burned my natural power out.

Tristan must have sensed my withdrawal, for he released me.

"How do you find your quarters?"

"Well, my lord."

"Are you hungry? I wouldn't want our guest to find our hospitality lacking."

I shook my head, knotting my hands together. The bowl of figs still sat on the table, but I could not eat them now. They were Lars' gift. The juice, the sweetness would all remind me of him, and his kiss.

Why had the spell stripped me of so much, to leave me at the mercy of the mating heat? Why had the Goddess allowed it? Did she not hear our prayers to defeat the Corpse King? Or was I unworthy?

"Come. I will show you something."

He led me from the rooms, and I was too preoccupied to protest. A labyrinth of halls, and then we emerged outdoors, just within the castle walls. Warriors milled about the keep. They turned as one as Tristan led me past. I kept the veil over my hair, but it was no matter. I was the only woman, and to them, my scent must seem the sweetest treat. I knew from my time that the Berserkers could scent a spaewife. My body sang a siren song to them.

We came to an empty yard, and a set of stone stairs leading to the top of the wall. Tristan's cloak blew in the wind as he ascended.

"What is it you wish to show me?" I hesitated on the final step. He could take me up here to throw me off.

He stood at the edge and beckoned. "Nervous? I will not let you fall."

His challenge decided for me. I boldly stepped up to the edge of the wall. Shouts wafted up to us, along with cries and clanks of axe and sword meeting shield. In the field below, warrior faced warrior.

"They spar." Tristan nodded to his men, and I edged closer.

One giant stood in the center of a circle of men,

roaring and challenging all who came near. Challengers advanced and he repelled them all, his booming laugh echoing off the stones. He seemed familiar, but it could not be...

"Is that—?"

"The warrior you saved."

"He's already well?"

Tristan nodded slowly.

"You doubt your own powers?"

"I have no powers," I said, watching the great warrior charge two men, meeting their axes and blades with his own.

"You believe this." Tristan's brow furrowed.

I shrugged. "I used to be very powerful. I am no longer."

The commander turned back to the fine fighting below. "You're powerful enough."

On the practice field, the battle mad warrior twisted, disarming one of his opponents with a shout. He kicked the fallen axe away, and turned his assault the remaining challenger, who fell within seconds.

Victory cries rose from the field and warriors beat their shields. The great warrior, prisoner no more, looked up where his commander and I stood, his red cloak and my white garb fluttering in the fierce wind.

"Lady," the battlements rang with his cry. "A token."

My heart fluttered as all the warriors turned to behold me, but my eyes were only for the greatest fighter of them all. I had nothing of my own to give. Tugging free my hair cloth, I let the wind take it from my hands to his, where he brought it to his lips and pressed it to his heart.

I waited a moment, my hair crackling in the wind like a bright flag. Then I turned and followed Tristan as he led me away.

On the last step I tripped and almost fell. Tristan caught me and cursed. "You need food."

"No." I had fasted for this journey, eaten only honey. My body was stronger than this.

"You will obey me," he told me gruffly.

I pulled myself from his arms and gave a mock curtsey. It had been many a year since I'd been so weak I must yield to a man.

"Stubborn woman," he muttered as he drew me along. He didn't take me to my rooms, but to a low structure near the wall, outfitted with a long table and benches and filled with the smell of roasting meat.

A familiar swarthy warrior stood as we came in.

"Ivar," Tristan greeted him, "Where is Lars?"

"About to face the challenger on the field." To my surprise, the bearded warrior bowed to me. "Well done, lady."

I bit my lip against protesting that I had done little. The truth was, I didn't know what I'd done. I had a little power, subtle, latent. I did not know how to use it or what it was worth.

"Weak, frail things often have more power than we know," Ivar said as if reading my thoughts.

I stared at him, and he cocked his head, a small smile on his lips. The worry had left his face, making him look younger, almost as young as Lars, and handsome. Heat swirled through me, a giddy warmth that rose and fell, and rose again when Tristan touched my arm and had me sit on the bench.

Tristan rapped on a small wooden door above a counter. "Food for one."

"You're feeding her the warrior's mess?" Ivar raised a brow.

Tristan growled in response, something along the lines of, "Better this than what might be provided," and Ivar nodded a response.

The door scraped open and the smell of food hit me hard. I stared at the table's wood grain, wondering if my stomach would settle. I would blame my unease on the spell, the Corpse King's magic, and the events of the day, but in truth I was unsettled by the proximity of so many handsome warriors. It had been many years since I had feelings like these—so long I didn't remember. I was but a girl when I joined the acolytes and began my training, and not worldly. Initiates were expected to be pure. Men did not turn our heads, and though I had dallied with warriors—Berserkers in my own time—I had never felt this way.

I risked a glance at Ivar. The warrior offered me a kind look, as if he knew my struggle. I wished I had my magic. I could gather it around me like a shield. I'd feel myself again, if I could hide.

Tristan plunked down a plate. "Eat."

I stared at the food—dried figs, meat stew, and a few rounds of bread.

"It's good," Ivar said, using his own bread to mop up the gravy. He leaned back in his chair as I tried to swallow the lump in my throat. "How goes our guest's visit, commander?"

When Tristan didn't answer, I raised my eyes to Ivar's dark ones. "I am to meet the king."

Tristan growled, sounding more beast than man. Ivar looked at him sharply.

The commander sat down beside me, picking up a piece of bread and tearing it. "After this we will bring you to bathe and prepare for your audience. Tonight, you will dine with him."

I twisted my hands in my gown. I didn't know it would be so soon. I thought I'd have time to prepare, not that I had much I could to do.

After a minute, Tristan sighed. "Lady," he scooted closer, offering the bread.

I shook my head.

"Let me," Ivar said.

"Very well," Tristan rose. "I must go make sure half my warriors haven't fallen to our champion on the practice field. Deliver her to the baths."

The air grew heavy as Tristan left us alone. I watched Ivar warily as he sat down next to me. He'd disapproved of Lars flirting with me, but the smile between the close-cropped beard told me he wasn't feeling so stern anymore.

"Start with a fig." He held it up until I opened my mouth. Then he fed it to me.

"It is good, is it not? We receive wagons of tribute. I'm told they dry on the way here." He picked up another tidbit.

"Next is a honey cake. Come, it is Lars favorite. His mother favored them, and he remembers her."

Between bites, I asked, "Do you remember your mother?"

"Sometimes. I dream of her." He kept his lips pressed tight as he fed me more.

"I never met her. She died in childbirth. Lars' mother nursed me, and she is who I remember."

He started to offer a cake to me, and when I darted my head forward to take it, he whipped it away and took a bite instead, winking at me. "Because of her, I am also fond of honeycakes."

I smiled at his playfulness. He brushed some crumbs from my gown.

"Do you eat meat?"

I shook my head.

"Pity. I am a fine hunter."

"So humble," I teased.

He laughed, and it warmed my heart. When we first met, Ivar seemed so serious. I wondered what had changed.

"I caught you easily enough" he reminded me.

"I was not running. If I had, you would've found victory much harder to win."

"I hope, then, you never run from me."

Our eyes met, and heat flashed through my body again, as if he'd touched me. He had his own set of Gifts, though I did not know what they were. And would never know, if I completed my task and left at dawn.

The thought made me sad.

As if he sensed my change of feelings, he turned sober. For a while we were silent, he toyed with his cup.

"You're very brave to come here."

"I had no choice." I didn't admit why I was here. To do so would mean my death. If any of the Berserkers suspected treason, I'd be imprisoned and tortured. Who would wield the final executioners axe—Tristan? Ivar? Or the giant warrior I had saved?

"The man on the field..." I hesitated until Ivar nodded for me to continue. "What's his name?"

"Did he tell you?" Ivar's dark eyes bored into me.

"When I met him, he couldn't not remember."

"I wager he remembers now. Or will, after a few hours of sparring clears his head. If he did not tell you, then it's not for me to say." Ivar offered me another bite, and when I shook my head, he dusted off his hands and rose. "Come. It's time to visit the baths."

15

LARS

The warrior across from me wore no helm or armour but rushed in as if his skin would deflect a blade. I charged to meet him. Sword met sword with a clang that set my ears ringing. I grunted under the weight of my larger comrade, feet scrabbling in the dust. He was bigger, but I was faster. Letting my knees bend, I dropped out from under his crushing girth, and darted away, my sword nicking his leg as I passed. A rage-filled bellow filled the air.

Warily, I whirled to face my opponent. With relief, I noted he was smiling.

"First blood, Lars," the watching warriors shouted with respect. My opponent nodded his agreement, signaling the end of the sparring match.

"Well fought," he called. I grinned back and cleaned my sword as he leaned on his to catch his breath. One hand rubbed his wrist, which still bore a mark of a shackle.

"It was a good match," I agreed, approaching him. He stood, looming over even me, who was counted tall among the Berserkers. "Although I admit, it could've gone either way. Tomorrow you may yet beat me."

He grunted, and I stepped closer, lowering my voice. "It is good to have you back."

"It is good to be back. I admit I am surprised. The beast rose up," he shook his head. "I thought it was the end."

"It was... until she came." I did not need to mention the lady Yseult by name.

"She touched me," his voice held awe. "One touch and my mind cleared."

"Lars," someone called, and I turned to the commander crossing the field. We saluted him, my opponent included, and Tristan gave him a special salute before singling me out to follow him.

"Commander," I asked, wiping my sweaty face on my shirt as he stopped in the cool shade of the wall. "What brings you here? Where is the lady?"

"The king wishes to see her tonight."

"Tonight?" I repeated. I'd thought we'd have more time.

The frustration on Tristan's face told me the same. In the past, we'd worked together to protect maids from our king's scrutiny. Never defying him outright, just protecting the women he might prey upon. Women like our mother.

But this time it was not to be. Yseult was too special to escape notice.

"Gaul," I said, and Tristan nodded. The king's own spy within the guard's ranks. It would do well for him to meet an accident while we're on patrol—or on the practice field.

"Gaul must've passed news on to our liege. Yseult's audience is tonight. The king will take her to bride and then..." he shook his head. He knew as well as I what happened to the king's wives.

On the practice field, the greatest warrior among us

laughed as he sparred with six men at a time. Hours before he'd been a raving mad man.

Whoever this lady was, she held the key to our sanity. Our salvation. After decades of waiting, growing weary under the Berserker curse, we finally had hope.

"We must save her," I whispered.

"We must," Tristan agreed fiercely. "But how?"

16

YSEULT

var led me back into the castle, down halls that twisted and turned until I despaired of ever finding my way back to any room I knew. The mage might well use magic to keep the halls of his home too confusing for guests to memorize. A labyrinth, another layer of defense.

At last we came to a great marble entrance. The air was softer here, humid. Our footsteps echoed.

"In here," Ivar stepped aside and let me go first. I gasped at the long pool set in the middle of the room, surrounded by pillars and tiled walls. High, high above the pool, windows just under the great vaulted ceiling let in a little light. Swirls of color drew my eye, murals rivaling any picture I'd ever seen.

"This is beautiful," I gasped.

"Very beautiful," he smiled, but he seemed more pleased to watch me. "The baths are heated by deep earth springs. Enjoy yourself, lady," he bowed. "I will send another to fetch you."

Grateful for a moment alone, I padded to the pool and

leaned over the still water. My reflection peered back at me. I looked younger, softer somehow. Over the years, the magic I'd worked had made me, molded me. The Yseult gazing back at me from the waters was a simple maiden, untouched by any artifice. Could she face someone as powerful as the Corpse King?

I crouched down, gazing at the water. I wished it was a scrying glass that could give me some hint of my future. I don't know how long I sat, but when my reflection blended with another's, I looked up.

Tristan stood over me, his brow furrowed. "You did not bathe."

I rested my head against my knees, my dry state my only replace.

"Do you find this place pleasing?" He looked around the room as his voice echoed between the murals.

"It's peaceful. Who built these baths?"

"The Romans. They made the murals, too."

"Amazing. They are a grand empire." I did not tell him that in a thousand years, their baths would be a memory, the murals chipped and their roads crumbling. So much greatness faded to dusk. "Does your liege seek to rival them?"

"He already does. But let us not speak of him," Tristan set down his helm and gestured to the water. "You must ready yourself."

"I have nothing to wear."

"Garments are being prepared."

"By whom?"

He shook his head.

"Did you send to the village? Speak to a warrior who found me these?" I lifted a foot and pulled off the boots he'd given me, letting them fall with a thump.

He shook his head and turned to study the wall.

"Where are all the king's servants?"

"We serve at the pleasure of the king."

"I mean his court. Why is this place so empty?"

He angled his head enough for me to see he raised a brow. "You do not delight in our company?"

"You know I do." I imbued my voice with all my latent passion.

That made him turn, frustration on his face.

"Bathe," he ordered. "Make ready. And then I will tell you about the king."

"You will?"

"I had come to warn—" he broke off. "I have come to tell you what to expect when you meet with my liege."

I sucked in a breath. "Why?"

His shoulders rose, fell. "I wish to protect you."

I padded to him. It took everything in me not to put my hand along the side of his face, feel the rough edge of his stubbled jaw under my palm. "Why?" He was a Berserker, pledged to his lord. Why would he help me?

"I have never met anyone like you. My lady, please..."

"You call me lady. You know I am not."

"I know not what you are," his voice came out hoarse.

"I am but a maid," I said with full honesty. I'd seen my reflection in the pool. In this world, in this time, I was only myself. No magic, no artifice.

He stared over my head. "You are more than what you seem."

"Very well. I will bathe. If..." I hesitated, risking all. "If you will join me."

His eyes widened.

"Bathe with me, Tristan."

I backed away but waited until his nod before fussing with my garment, pulling it over my head and letting it fall.

Tristan had turned to study the murals. He would not look on my naked form. I smiled at his restraint.

Eagerly, I entered the water, warmed by the springs in the earth. I kicked around, sending ripples wide, splashing until I heard Tristan's armor fall.

I watched him strip off his warrior's garb. His muscles flexed, long arms and powerful legs, a great firm chest all revealed to my gaze. When he only wore a loincloth, his eyes fell on mine. I looked away at the last, blood rushing to my cheeks.

The water sighed as he entered the pool, and I again watched his dark head and broad shoulders come toward me.

"Is this what you wanted, lady?"

"Yes," I mouthed the word but had no breath to give it life. We swam in large circles around each other.

"I am glad of your hospitality," I said to Tristan. "Thank you for your escort."

Tristan hesitated. "What do you know of the mage?"

He said he'd protect me, but our trust was fragile and new. For all he knew, I was a spy. I would have to go very carefully. "I know he is very powerful. His reach increases every year."

Tristan nodded. "He is of old."

"The lore in my country tells of a king who wished to be strong to stand against his enemies. He had many wives and many sons. He wished for more power. He grew too strong and was said to be cursed by the gods." I bit my lip, waiting for Tristan to read the meaning behind my words.

"It is true. He gains power from the dark arts."

"He is a sorcerer," I whispered. I knew how the mage gained his power. Sacrifice.

"I do not want you to go to him," Tristan said, and the frustration in his voice made my eyes widen.

"You are the commander of his army."

"And spent my life pledged to his service along with my warrior brothers. But what have we gained but a long, endless descent into madness?"

"Would you betray him then?"

"If I did, I must have a reason. Some higher purpose. Something to live for."

I swallowed. I could barely meet his gaze.

He reached out, slowly, as if I were a bird that might fly away. Gently he tugged a wet lock of my hair. "Something... or someone."

"Tristan," I whispered. He kept playing with my hair, not meeting my eyes. "When I first saw you, I felt I'd known you forever."

"I dreamed of you, lady."

I moved forward, letting the water lap between us. "Mine was more than a dream. It felt like...a memory."

"Ivar says there is a woman foretold to become our mate."

I smiled. "You'd share me with your men?"

He met my gaze then, eyes flashing. "Not just any man. But my captains, we are more than comrades. More than brothers."

"From where I'm from, Berserker warriors mate in pairs. There are so few women to be their mates, and the companionship of their warrior brother allows them to fight the curse far longer. But, Tristan, you've known me but a day. Not even that long."

"I've known you since I first dreamed of your face. You

saved my brother from his fate. He would've succumbed to the battle madness, if not for you. You saved him." He stepped closer, and I was never more aware of a man. Everything in my body was tuned to him, strained towards him.

"Yseult, you saved us all."

I tilted my face upwards, feeling his breath on my lips. A beautiful moment, and then it was gone. Harsh footsteps and echoing voices made me cringe. Tristan stepped in front of me as warriors burst into view—Lars and Ivar, chasing down Gaul. I crossed my arms in front of my breasts and crouched behind the large commander, peering around his arm.

Lars and Ivar got in front of Gaul at the last, and stood shoulder to shoulder, weapons in hand, blocking him from coming further.

"Let me through. I have news from the king."

"What news?" Tristan's voice boomed.

Gaul craned his head "Where—" he started.

Lars pushed him back. "You will go no further."

"State your message," Ivar ordered.

The upstart warrior glared at them both. "The king has sent gifts to his guest. They are in her chambers."

"She sends thanks in reply," Tristan said. "Now leave us."

Gaul retreated, then stopped. "Take care commander, that you do not touch what is not yours."

"Enough," Lars pushed forward, knocking Gaul back. Ivar stopped his warrior brother with a hand on the blond's shoulder.

The three left, as quickly as they'd come.

Tristan cursed.

Before I could lift a hand to touch and soothe him, he strode away, leaving the pool, letting water stream off his naked form.

By the time I emerged, he was dressed, helmet and all. My heart ached. All my life I'd been alone, and satisfied, complete in my own power. But I needed this man like no other. His closeness, his touch, his strength lent to me so I could face the greatest threat of my life.

"Tristan—"

He faced the murals again and would not turn. "It was wrong of me to bathe with you. I will not take advantage again."

"You—"

"I am the king's commander. You are his guest. It will not happen again."

I bit my tongue. I wanted to rage and scream. I had but one day to do my duty, if I could. At the end, I would either live, or die.

But now I was not ready to die. Not without telling all my secrets to this man who seemed to know so much about me already.

I'd left my shift crumpled on the floor, but now it lay smooth and unwrinkled on a bench. The sight of the soft linen gave me pause. A faint scent of lavender lingered on the cloth, as if it'd been laundered and dried. But I had seen no servant come or go.

He has no need of human servants... but no one said anything about inhuman ones

Swallowing my worry, I slipped the now clean garment back on.

Tristan led me back to my rooms. I crossed to pour wine, pretending to be fine.

"What sort of women does the king prefer?" I asked in a nonchalant tone. I hoped to find some answers of what I would face tonight. If the Corpse King found me pleasing, this charade would continue. The spells I'd felt at the gate oppressive. He was certainly strong enough to kill me. If not by magic, he'd give the word and Tristan would run me through. The commander of the guard had no choice. "Well? You have served him many years. Does he prefer dark hair or blonde?"

Tristan had remained in the shadow on the edges of the room. "The king has no one preference that I know. He likes women whose essence lights the stone."

"Have you met many of his consorts?"

"Our mothers were all his wives."

Of course. I'd forgotten that part of the tale. The king took spaewives to his bed and sired an army of Berserkers. In the tales he also sacrificed his children.

I shuddered.

"You do not call him 'father.'"

Tristan shrugged. "He is the king."

"What a rich king, with so many heirs," I murmured, but knew the awful truth. The mage sought immortality. Ventured into the dark arts, his power eating his mind as much as the Berserkers lost theirs to the spell that made them. The king did not want heirs. He would live forever.

"If the king chooses you, he will make you into the bride he wishes you to be."

"Even if that is not my will?"

Tristan didn't answer.

I sank into a chair. The throbbing in my head was back. The Corpse King's magic weighing on me.

"You should rest," he turned away.

My only armor was the lack of magic. He would not recognize me as a threat. Of course, I had no way of defending myself

I would've trembled, but I'd been trained in the way of the initiates. The witch trials had driven all weakness from me. Of course, in my new magic stripped state, my body did not remember. But my mind did. Closing my eyes, I stilled myself.

And saw a great, bloody battlefield, stretching from my feet to the dying sun. Crows feasted on the bodies of warriors—all dead.

"Lady." My eyes snapped open. Lars was there, looming over me, looking more serious than I'd ever seen. "You have not examined your gifts." He swept out a hand towards the gown lying over the back of the couch. On the table there was a jeweled goblet and pitcher of wine.

"The king is very kind," I said. Lars' eyes widened at the bitterness in my voice. It didn't matter. Tristan had made his choice: remain loyal to the king. He and his warriors could kill me for disrespect, I no longer cared.

"He expects you at dusk."

"He dines so early?"

The blond inclined his head yes.

I went to the gown. "It is beautiful."

Lars still hovered at the door. "It will look lovely on you."

I held up the garment, turning it this way and that. It was shot through with threads of gold. Against the shimmering fabric, my own white shift looked so plain.

"No," I laid the gown down. "No. Let him look on me as I am." At least my shift was clean.

"You reject the king's gifts?"

"I do not want to wear them. Let him see me as I am."

"You are brave, lady. Very brave or very foolish."

"Perhaps I am both."

I crossed to the fountain to check my reflection in the dying light. The white garb I'd worn for the ceremony was meant to symbolize purity. In it I looked like a fresh maiden. I had stopped aging long ago, when the magic I handled gave me an artificial youth. But this was different. In the fresh shift, stripped of my powers, I truly looked young, virginal.

It was madness to think I'd be a match for a powerful mage.

Goddess, help me.

Armor clanked behind me, but I didn't turn. Tristan spoke quietly. "It is time."

I followed him through the halls. Ivar and Lars brought up the rear. We entered a long hall, with great windows that let in the day's final light. The shadows lay strangely between the columns, rippling and flickering. Dark tendrils rising up as if trying to reach for me. Out of the corner of my eye I caught them following us. I fisted my hands in my shift and forced myself to scurry on.

Tristan slowed as we approached giant gilt doors, stretching above us to the cavernous ceiling, tall as ten men.

"Lady," a voice rasped at my right. A warrior stepped from the shadows. Lars steadied me while Tristan moved to block him.

"Wait," I put a hand on Tristan's bicep. I recognized the third warrior from the dungeon. He stood tall and proud again, his helm shining and face clear. No dark magic buzzed around his head.

"I remember," he said. "You asked my name, and now I remember. It is Magnus. That is the name my mother gave me."

"Well met, Magnus," I smiled up at him, pushing Tristan gently out of my way so I could stand before the large man. "Remember your mother. Remember her and be whole."

"Lady," he bowed, backing into the shadows once more.

I stepped in front of the great doors.

"Ready?" Tristan asked, not meeting my eyes. He was

sure he was delivering me to death. If not tonight, then one day.

I took a deep breath. "I am."

Lars and Ivar took their place at either door and opened them slowly. Air rushed out, along with faint whispers. My skin prickled as magic licked over me.

I forced myself to take a few steps. Inside stretched a great hall, again lined with windows tall as an oak. But these windows let in nothing but darkness.

I hesitated and almost backed into Tristan. He stood at my back, steadying me, and did not urge me forward. Across the great expanse of the room, a low light lit a dais where I knew the king would be waiting.

"I'm ready," I repeated, and went forward again.

Just inside the doors, I sensed him stop. "I can go no further." he told me. I nodded.

"Have care, lady." He backed away and bowed, dusky light gleaming off his helm until the doors swung shut. Tristan would remain on the other side, waiting for my return. The thought bolstered me as I crossed the echoing flagstones.

The journey seemed to take an age, but finally I stopped at the foot of the stairs leading to the dais. A table was there, bare, with only one chair available. But of the king, there was no sign. I wanted to shiver in the heavy quiet, but I made myself still, made myself wait.

You are not wearing my gifts. The voice rang around me, a rich timbre that caressed my limbs, quickened my heart.

I stopped in my tracks, letting the magic snake around me, tasting me.

The dais was still empty. The Corpse King had not shown himself.

I opened my mouth, hesitated.

Speak, the command hung on the air.

I curtseyed. "Forgive me my lord. Your gifts were so fine. I am a simple maid. I felt I did not deserve them."

"No?" amusement. "Most women love my gifts."

I curtsied again. "The king may have whatever woman he pleases."

"You wonder why I would pick you?" Wind wafted through the hall, lifting my hair, making my shift swirl around my ankles. "You have beauty enough."

"Thank you, my lord."

"Come closer, girl."

Heart beating, I ascended the dais.

Shadow shimmered, became solid, I didn't look at it directly at first. Then movement behind me caught my eye. I turned and didn't stop my gasp

The mage was tall, much taller than any man, even the Berserkers he made. Thinner too, a lean build, he wore robes that did not hide his broad shoulders. Not a soldier, a scholar. A ruler.

"Welcome, Yseult. Welcome to my home."

17

TRISTAN

I stared at the doors to the king's audience chamber, my hands curled to fists.

"You did well, commander," Gaul's voice snaked around me. "Now run along, back to your post."

The king's sentinel stood behind me with two large Berserkers. I recognized them, but they were not my own. The madness had taken their minds long ago, but they obeyed Gaul.

I wondered how many in my own ranks were like these dumb servants, and how long it would take to fight them.

"Did you hear me, commander? You're dismissed."

I stared at him for a moment. I could not explain that I had to wait to see if the woman I loved would return. But I would not be driven from my post like a dog.

"Your duty to the king is over," he said, and it was. I served the king no longer.

I served Yseult.

"Commander?" Magnus rumbled at my back. He and Ivar and Lars waited for my orders. They would fight alongside me. They loved our lady as much as I did.

"Come. I wish to speak to you," I said and started to march away. Gaul snickered as I passed.

I turned and drove my fist into his face. He snapped back, bouncing off the impassive Berserker slaves, and fell to the ground. I left him there and led my men to the shadows.

"Well done," Lars grinned. "I have wanted to do that for a long time."

Magnus chuckled, but Ivar looked worried.

"Tristan... Commander, have care. There are many who follow him."

"How many?" I asked. "Can you find out?"

Eyes wide with surprise, Ivar nodded.

"The wind is turning," I murmured. "We must be ready."

"We will be," Magnus said. "It will be our pleasure to serve our lady." He put his fist to his chest in salute. Ivar and Lars followed suit.

"Our lady," I echoed, and did the same. We would fight for her. We would die for her.

"You will watch, and watch, and heed my command," I cautioned.

"Commander," they agreed. Ivar and Lars left. Magnus and I turned to wait for our lady's return.

I hoped she pleased the king, so she would not die. But more than that I wished to claim her as my own.

If she survived, I would send her away. To the corners of the earth, or beyond. I would not let her stay.

Even if it cost my life.

18

YSEULT

He's charming, Tristan had said. Truth be told, I'd never met a more beautiful man. Sharp patrician features. Skin smooth as polished stone, pale and stretched over the fine bones of his face. A face that would turn heads in a market square, even without the aura of power that cloaked the massive figure.

I was used to the strange beauty magic bestowed on its long-time users. After many years my own face took on the otherworldly polish, growing almost inhumanly attractive. I'd forgotten what my own face looked like until I woke up this morning in a field, and looked in the water cup at my old, youthful face.

I expected the Corpse King's charm. I braced for it. What I did not expect was for him to look so like Tristan. The commander was right. Whatever the Berserker warriors were now, they'd been sired one way or another by the king they served.

"Will you sit, my dear?" the king asked, his long fingers wrapping around a chair's high back.

With a jerky nod, I crossed the rest of the way, twitching

my body into place like it was a puppet and I held the strings.

Up close, the Corpse King was even more striking. His lips held a bit of a smile, as if he knew how dazzled I was. I turned. Fortunately, I'd met Tristan, and could cling to that resemblance. Beside the mage, the commander would look homely, raw boned and rough. But Tristan's earthy beauty was real. The king's charm was all magic made. Breathtaking, but as alien as a star.

"Are you hungry?" the king asked.

"A little, my lord," I lied.

He waved a hand and a feast appeared.

I startled as if I'd never seen a spell before. The scent of roast boar hit me, making my stomach churn.

I felt he was smirking at me. With all my gaping and trembling, I must seem a very foolish maiden indeed. Perhaps he would think me simple and I would get through this unscathed.

"Eat then," He gestured to the table. "No need to keep to ceremony. It is only us." The king crossed to the other end of the table and sat down.

As he passed, I caught the scent of something putrid, rotten under the cloying scent of myrrh. As if I'd walked past an open tomb. The stench made me blink, and then it was gone.

I tasted its memory at odds with his seductive voice and glittering good looks.

I took a small loaf of bread off a platter and toyed with it. All the while watching the king without looking at his face like a rabbit waiting for a snake to strike. Just because it pleases the snake to act as if it will not attack, doesn't mean the prey can let down its guard.

"Have my men treated you well?" His voice made me jump.

"Yes, my lord. Well enough."

"Did they question you?"

"Yes. But realized I was harmless."

"Not many maidens stray close to my home. I have a reputation. Plenty of women are sent by their villages to curry favor. I suppose that is why you have come." He paused. "You are not eating."

I picked up the bread and nibbled at it. I half expected it to be a magical food that seduced my senses same as the Corpse King's looks, but it tasted like real bread, even as it turned to dust in my nervous mouth.

He gestured to his empty plate. "I am not hungry, but I have a terrible thirst."

A clinking sound made me twist in my seat. A pedestal with a glass carafe and large, bejeweled cup had appeared. My spine prickled.

"Shall I serve you, my lord?" Tremors had begun to run up my legs. Something wasn't right.

"No need." As I watched, the carafe lifted as if by unseen hands. Thick red liquid poured into the gem encrusted goblet.

The rubies flashed among the dull gold as it passed through the air, drifting by me on its way to the king. I caught another flash of the awful stench.

"Forgive me. I've forgotten my manners. Are you thirsty? Would you like a sip?"

I shook my head. Something told me whatever was in that cup, it was more than red wine. It should not pass my lips.

And then I saw them, lying in wait in the shadows beyond the throne. Women. Hordes of them, lovely and silent, dressed in robes that left their arms bare. Their hair up in elaborate coiffures, their garments those of a queen.

They were all watching me. One rested her hands on her large belly, as if she was still pregnant.

Any appetite I had fled.

"Did my men explain to you what an honor it is to be my consort?"

Not taking my eyes from the ghost women, I answered. "They said you have your pick of women. You require the villages to send any eligible maidens, and you keep many of them as wives."

"Only the most beautiful." His smile turned my stomach.

"Where are they?" I asked, even though I knew.

"They all die young. Tragic."

The watching ghosts moved then, a ripple through their ranks.

"All of them?" I whispered.

"Some soon after bearing my children. Others linger but catch a wasting disease. Sooner or later, they all succumb." he shrugged. "And so I am left all alone."

"And your children?"

"All sons. Some live to adulthood. More die like their mothers."

"That's horrible," I rasped.

"Yes."

"And so I am left alone." Alone, alone, alone, his voice echoed, a shivering wind running through the hall. The ghost women didn't move. Some looked at their king with contempt.

"So you see, Yseult," his voice wrapped around my body, winding like a chain. "I am searching for the one woman who can withstand my power. Who can stay healthy and well. She will rule beside me as queen. Forever."

A fire burned in his eyes, but I could see nothing but the silent ranks of women. Their eyes gave warning. *Run, get away while you still can.*

My chest struggled to rise under the weight of whatever spell the Corpse King had wrapped around me. Even now the voice kept chanting in my ear. *So beautiful, so young. Taste the power. You will be a queen.* The thoughts filled my head.

No. I will not. I am... In a panic, I realized I could not remember my name.

Tristan, I cried silently. *Lars, Ivar. Magnus.* I recalled their faces both dark and fair, bearded and clean shaven. These men were real. So rough, so wild, so hungry for love. How could I tell them who I was? How could I be with them when I was leaving on the morn?

"Yseult," the Corpse King said. My head jerked up, he was standing over me, the shadows lay in the hollows of his face. He looked suddenly like a skeleton. All his beauty fell away. He was a monster, something called up from the grave.

I looked for the ghosts of his wives, but they were gone. Banished. The silence screamed where they'd been.

"You are more than what you seem," the Corpse King's voice reached my ears without his lips moving.

"I... don't know what you mean," I whispered.

"You please me." His long, bony fingers came to my face and it took all my self-control not to flinch away. "I have not met a woman like you... in a long, long time."

His eyes burned into me and suddenly I could not draw breath.

My lungs screamed for air. As if remembering, he snapped his fingers, and the chain around my chest loosened. I gasped, sagging.

"I will summon you again, tonight. You will come and obey me."

I nodded, mute. What else could I do?

His fingers drifted back towards my face. Had I ever thought him beautiful, he was no more than a skeleton and burning eyes, the skin stretched over his skull. His fingers carried the stench from the cup he drank, a sharp iron smell, mixed with spices used to purify graves.

"So young," he crooned, his deep voice a caress. "So lovely."

As bony fingers squeezed my shoulders, I struggled not to pull away. A sharp squeeze his hand at my neck. His touch burned like cold fire.

His lips found my ear.

"Tonight, wear the garment I sent you."

And he disappeared.

Wrenching myself out of my seat, I flew down the dais steps, past the place where the ghosts had gathered, and fled from the hall.

Soft mocking laughter echoed around me, but other than that, the only sound was my frantic footsteps and harsh breathing.

I had a moment of panic as I struggled to open the large, heavy doors

"No," I gasped. "Let me out."

I fought to heave them open a crack and struggled through to the other side, staggering in my haste to get away.

The two silent guards stood on either side, not moving to help me. I stumbled and righted myself, taking flight once more. The air was different on this side of the doors, fresh and inviting. I'd been kept in a tomb and set free.

Rushing, I clutched a pillar to keep from falling, and

retched what little I'd eaten on the floor. Still the guards did not move, but I ran in case they called me back.

"Yseult?"

I did not stop even when a large armored figure stepped out in front of me.

"Yseult?"

Tristan caught me in his arms. I fought him, thrashing.

"Yseult, it's me," he carried me away from the throne room, into the shadows beyond the massive columns.

His worried face flashed before my eyes. Reminding me of the women I'd seen. The familiar faces. Oh Goddess, I'd seen the wives. The ghosts.

"Get me away from here," I shrieked.

"It's all right, you're safe," Tristan crooned. He smelled like the outdoors, the grasses and trees and everything real.

I was crying.

"We're leaving. Come." The further he carried me, the more I saw through the cobwebs the mage's spell had wound around my mind. The king had almost enthralled me but let me go to toy with me. I was not strong enough to face him, and I was to return.

What was I to do?

"No, shhh, lady," Tristan soothed, and I realized I was crying. He set me down. I clung to him, but he kept me in his lap, sliding one large hand up and down my back. "Please don't cry," he murmured, like a mother with child.

Goddess, all those murdered women. The mage took them to wife, and then drained their powers. If he had his way, I'd be next.

"Tristan," I whispered. The warrior locked his arms around me, his warmth seeping into my numb limbs. I clung to him.

I'd been blasted back in time to learn the secrets of

defeating the mage. But without my magic, I was as helpless as the ghosts of the Corpse King's wives. I could no longer go on alone.

"Tristan," I tipped back my head to search his face, and as I did the heat flared between us. Whatever it was, he felt it too. He cupped my cheeks and kissed me.

The floodgates opened. A lifetime of suppressing all emotion, all my strict training swept away. I pressed myself against Tristan's hard chest, my hands frantically tugging him closer, as if he were a rock I clung to in the storm.

At last, I broke away with a moan. My body was full of molten desire, no longer my own.

"Do not ask me to take you to him again," Tristan said fiercely against my lips. "I will not. I cannot."

A cool wind blew around us, whispers rising in the dark. I remembered myself, where I was, and pushed him away. "I must," I whispered. "The king wishes me to come to him again."

Tristan cursed. "When?"

"Tonight."

Still cursing, he ran his hand through his thick hair. He'd brought me back to the women's chambers. We were seated on a low couch. Rising, he paced to a table and brought back a cup of something.

"Drink this."

It was water, and I blessed its cool comfort. Tristan settled his great body beside mine. We weren't touching but his heat enveloped me the same.

"You must tell me everything. What happened? What did you see?"

"I saw the mage, the king."

"He was there? He did not just speak from the air?"

"At first he did. Then he showed himself to me."

I stared at my cup, remembering the ghosts. Even now I felt them rustling about their old chambers. Until I knew their intent, I dare not speak of them, and call them further into this realm from their own.

"I'm sorry I didn't warn you more."

"Tristan," I raised my eyes to his. "I have to tell you something." He was the king's commander. If I confessed treason, his duty was to run me through.

But he'd kissed me. More than flirtation. More than the games I'd played with Lars. Tristan's kiss had cleared my mind.

"I am more than what I seem—" I began, when men's voices echoed through the room.

"It's all right," Tristan soothed when I startled. "It's just Ivar and Lars."

And Magnus, though he stayed by the door, lingering in the shadows with weapon drawn. He stood a head taller than all the rest.

"Lady," Lars came to me, his face lit with eagerness. "We are glad of your return. We have something to show you."

At Tristan's nod, he took my hands and helped me up, then led me to the courtyard, where I was struck dumb. There were white blooms everywhere I looked, bundles of them placed around the fountain, petals floating in the water.

"We wished to honor you," Tristan murmured.

I smiled through my tears.

"We found them by the north wall." Lars plucked a bloom and gave it to me. "Moonflower. They bloom in darkness."

"They're beautiful. You must have picked them all."

"I hadn't noticed them before today. They appeared near our sparring field soon after you walked the castle wall, and bloomed soon after dusk," Ivar said. "They only bloom one night."

"My mother used to say, 'There can be good in the world if flowers can still bloom,'" Lars added.

"Thank you." I could barely speak. Somehow, someway, these men cared for me.

And even if they did not, I could keep my secrets no longer. Better to tell them and risk their wrath then have the Corpse King enthrall me in his power.

"I have something to tell you. All of you."

"Not here," Tristan said. Taking my arm, he guided me back to the inner room, where he sat on the couch with me. The other three men arranged themselves about the room.

"I was a witch once. In a time and place far from here. A thousand years to be exact." I gave them a moment to absorb this. "I was born with powers, natural magic, the gift from the Goddess. But I chose another path." I glanced around at the waiting faces. "All magic requires sacrifice. Small spells, a small sacrifice. A bit of blood or bone. Larger spells require greater sacrifice. Over my lifetime, I have sacrificed much for power."

"What did you sacrifice?" Magnus' voice boomed in the dark.

"Nothing like the mage. No. I am not a murderer. Sorcery is an abomination." The ghost's whispers swirled around me. A breeze tugged the edge of my shift. "I gave up my natural abilities and trained with the witches. We sacrificed animals—mice, goats, doves. Their pain and death grew my powers. I became strong, stronger than any of my witch sisters. That is why I was chosen to face the mage.

"In our time, he was bound by a spell that made him sleep a thousand years, but now he is free, and threatens us all. I was sent to find a way to defeat him. I must learn the secrets of the binding spell and return to my sisters in my own time. That is why I am here." Slowly I raised my eyes to them. Four men, so different and so alike. Warriors all, pledged to the king, but perhaps... perhaps... the help the Goddess had sent to me.

Or not. If I had misread, they would either deliver me to the mage or strike a blow to end me.

"How will you find the spell?

"I don't know," I said in a choked voice. "When I arrived, something—the Corpse King's defenses or my sisters' spell —stripped me of all my powers. I cannot use magic to defend myself or to hide. That is how you caught me so easily," I said to Ivar, and he nodded.

"And now the king says I must return to him."

Ivar sighed. "He's decided he wants you as his bride."

I nodded. "If he takes me to wife, how long will I survive?"

"Not long," Ivar answered. "It depends. Some women weaken and die right away. Others bear him many sons. But after time, all of them perish. If not by his hand..." he trailed off and I answered for him.

"By his magic leaching their essence."

Tristan spoke up. "I can't let that happen. I won't."

"Shhh," I stopped his promises with my fingers on his lips. "You cannot. You are his commander, sworn to protect him. If he knew—"

He pulled down my hand and kissed it. "My life is yours."

"And mine," Magnus stepped from the shadows. Despite his great size, he moved swiftly and knelt close. "Along with my blade."

Lars and Ivar also knelt, murmuring the same.

I couldn't stop tears tracking down my face. "You don't even know me."

"We beheld you first in our dreams. You hold the power to free us from the battle rage," Tristan said.

"Our meeting was foretold," Ivar murmured.

I knew it was true. From the first, I felt I knew these men. I told them this, and their glad expressions broke my heart. These warriors would fight for me. But for naught. Against the mage's magic, they would die.

"We will find a way to stand against him," Tristan said. "You said he was trapped for a thousand years."

"Yes," I hesitated, then spoke my greatest fear. "But the lore said he was bespelled by one of his wives, who found a way to ensnare him, and joined her strength with all the others to stand against him."

"But he has no more wives," Ivar said.

I pressed my lips together. I did not know what it meant. Had my coming back in time changed the pattern of events?

A hard knock on the door drove the warriors to their feet. Sword drawn, Magnus opened it, and scowled at the one beyond.

"The king requests his lady at midnight." I recognized Gaul's voice.

I let my head sink into my hands. So soon. I had hoped for a reprieve, hoped he'd change his mind.

"Noted," Magnus said, and started to shut the door in the messenger's face. There was a struggle, and Gaul pushed his way into the room. His left eye was blackened from a fist, and even though Ivar and Lars blocked his way, his eyes landed on me with hate.

"I have more to say," Gaul spat in my direction. "She must dress in the clothes he sent to her. She must look like a queen. By order of the king."

"She will," Tristan said. "Now leave us." His voice cracked with power, and to my surprise, Gaul obeyed.

Magnus slammed the door behind the retreating warrior. "He grows bold," the giant warrior growled.

"We will deal with him," Tristan said. "And with those who follow him."

"I'll go with him now, and keep an eye on him," Magnus said, and bowing to me, left.

"Lady, you should rest. You don't have much time," Ivar said. "We will leave you alone." He tugged Lars arm. The blond darted forward, leaned down and gave me an impish kiss. "Till we meet again," he waggled his brows until I couldn't help but smile at both warrior's retreating backs.

Tristan leaned closer to me. His hand rested on my nape, and I winced. Frowning, he tugged away my gown and sucked in a breath.

"Lady, who has harmed you?"

Craning my neck, I noted the bruises livid on my skin. "The mage touched me." His hand had left a collar of bluish marks.

Tristan's whole body tensed, but his voice was cool. "Don't show Magnus. It will send him again into battle madness."

"Is Magnus fully healed?"

The anger emanating off the commander dimmed somewhat. "He is. Miracle of miracles."

"Out on the practice field he terrorized all who dare spar with him."

"That's Magnus," Tristan chuckled. "He will never be gentle, but thanks to you, he has his right mind. Truly a boon. A ray of sunlight on this dark day."

"Good," I closed my eyes as exhaustion washed through me.

"You should rest," Tristan made to leave, and I caught his hand.

"Please. Stay with me."

I curled against him. Slowly, as if afraid he might scare me away, his hand came to stroke back my hair.

"You don't have to do this, you know," he said when I was almost asleep.

"Hmm?"

"The four of us spoke. We can find a way to get you out."

I raised my head, no longer tired. They'd help me run. But then what would happen to them?

"I was sent to find a way to stop the Corpse King from destroying my people."

"Do you know how?"

"No. They should've sent another. One used to fighting without power. As it is, I do not know how to face him."

"So what then? You offer yourself up to him? What crime did you commit to be sacrificed so?"

I gazed at my hands.

Tristan cursed and kicked at the unlit brazier sending wood flying.

"And if it does no good?"

"I must try," I whispered.

"Why did they send you here with no weapons? With nothing to use against him?"

"I have my wits, my looks."

"Your innocence." He ran a hand through his hair. "You will be sacrificed on the mage's altar, and none of your people will even know what happened to you."

I prayed that would not happen.

His shoulders hunched, helpless. Even without his helm, commander's cloak, and armor, he was the picture of a powerful man, frustrated. For all his strength, he was unable to protect me.

I laid a hand on his arm. "I will be all right."

"Will you? Do you know what my king does to innocent women? He charms them. He takes them to bed. He keeps them in his harem and gets sons on them. And when he is done, he sacrifices them to build his power."

"You have seen him do this?"

"I have watched... too many. All our mothers. And then his children..."

I steadied myself. I'd heard horrible stories of how the mage treated his children. "What of his children?"

"All sons. We become his army. All half-brothers. We share a close bond. We also have great power."

"Until his magic drives you mad," I said. "In my time, we call the mage "The Corpse King.""

Tristan barked a bitter laugh. "We are his soldiers. We leave the corpses."

I put a hand on his arm to stop his self-censure. "You are an honorable man. The mage holds many in his thrall, in this time, and in my time, as the Corpse King." I did not tell him why we called him so. In my time, the Corpse King raised the dead so that they walked and served him, animated by the worst of evil magic—necromancy. "He will not stop until he has enslaved all of us. That is why my people fear. That is why I must face him. I must, Tristan, it's why I have come."

"Yseult." He cupped my face. I waited for his kiss, but he only held me, studying my face with sorrow marring his. "If I let you go, would you run?"

"No." But I let my gaze drop for I did not know my own fortitude. I hoped I would make the courageous choice.

"Then ready yourself. I will take you to him."

I prepared myself for the Corpse King's summons in the same way I had prepared for my sisters' spell. I bathed, not a full luxurious bath, but a quick one with a bowl of water and a bit of cloth. I used my shift to dry, and reluctantly shrugged on the gold gown. The king had sent slippers with his gifts, and after washing my feet, I put them on. I found a brush in one of the women's rooms. Saying a prayer for its owner, I attacked my hair, leaning over the fountain to peer at my reflection. Pale, with dark circles under my eyes, I looked like a ghost. My hair haloed around my head. Try as I might, I could not get it to fall flat.

Finally, I braided it down my back and wove in a few moonflowers. They released a strong scent when crushed, and for a time I played with them, enjoying my gift while I could. I'd never had a lover try to charm me.

"Lady," Tristan entered the courtyard, his helm under his arm. He slowed as he approached me, and touched a finger to my hair. "The most beautiful flowers bloom in darkness."

I let out a shaky breath. "From where I come from, I am not considered beautiful."

"Then your people are blind."

Or I hid my beauty behind my witch self, my strangeness, my power. "I wish we could've met sooner, then."

"Yseult, it's not too late to run."

"I cannot. My sisters are waiting for me, a thousand years back in time. I must find a way to defeat him and send the knowledge back. Even if I do not survive."

He drew me close, his lips at my forehead. "I cannot do this. I cannot bring you to him. Don't ask me."

I wrapped my arms around him, pushing up to press my cheek to his. I had never needed a man, but in this time, in this world, I needed Tristan like my lungs needed air. If I did not touch him. I would die.

"You must find a way to fight him," he said. I stayed silent, for I could not. I had no weapons.

Tristan drew out his talisman. "Take this. My mother thought it would protect her against him." The moonstone flashed in the darkness. "She gave it to me. I give it to you, lady. It is yours."

I nodded and bowed my head, so he could fasten it around my neck.

"I will return," I told him. "I will face the Corpse King and return."

A great shadow fell across us. Magnus, looming in the doorway.

"It is time."

19

YSEULT

Our march to the king's chambers took little time. All along the halls, Berserkers lined the way. I saw Gaul and a few of his followers scowling at me, but most of the faces were watchful, waiting.

At the gilt doors, Tristan halted. I turned with him to face my honor guard. "We go on from here alone."

Lars, Ivar, and Magnus all looked worried.

"I will be fine," I told them. At least I knew what I would face. The Corpse King might try to seduce me. If that failed he would try to use his magic to overwhelm me. He could easily rape my mind, leave me his slave, a shell of a woman he could use to bear his sons. He would absorb my spaewife magic if he could.

Somehow, I would fight.

Tristan guided me to the doors, which drew open without a touch and set the shadows whispering.

For a moment, I leaned into Tristan.

"Yseult," he breathed, and I willed him not to ask me to run. If he did, I would say yes. But it would mean his death, and mine. If he wished, the Corpse King could find us anywhere. There was no place we could go.

"I'm fine," I said. He studied me with dark eyes that saw more than I would have him see.

"Very well." He kissed my brow and withdrew. "Return to me."

My new gown swirling about my legs, I strode into the Corpse King's lair. My boldness lasted but a few steps, when I saw the long hall leading to a low dais, and a bed. Again, there was no sign of the Corpse King, but I slowed, my neck prickling. Someone was following me.

Halfway to the bed, I caught sight of the silvery shapes of women surrounding me. If I turned to look, they'd disappear into the shadows. The former wives, all ghosts.

Tonight, they were my companions, as well as a warning of what I could become.

"You wore the gifts I sent you." The rich voice in the dark, startled me. I stopped short. The king stepped into the room, wearing a mage's robe and a crown on his head. I dropped into a curtsey, and he waved a hand to call me to him, but I could not will my feet to move.

"You look lovely."

"Thank you."

"A queen. Worthy of a king." This time he raised a hand and an unseen force drew me forward. My heart pounded but I was frozen in the grip of magic. "You will rule beside me, Yseult. And whole worlds will fall at our feet."

He touched me, and I was no longer in his chambers. I stood on the battlements again, watching the Berserkers fight. This time they were not sparring, but marching forward, advancing to the far corners of the earth while the king and I watched.

The mage spoke in my ear, "With the power we have, none can stand in our way."

The vision fell away. The king turned me to face him, tipping my chin up. His touched burned a little, but in the face of his beauty, I was dazzled.

Tristan. Someone whispered. *Ivar. Lars. Magnus.*

Where did I know these names?

As the king held me, the ghosts rippled the air around us. *Our sons. They are our sons. Only you can save them.* Women's voices. The spaewives.

"It is time," the mage said. His deep voice rolled over me, pulling me under. He took my wrist, tugging me towards the bed. My mind rebelled even as my body followed.

Yseult, the ghosts whispered. *The necklace. Use the stone.*

Necklace? I'd forgotten. My free hand went to my breast where the stone lay nestled between them. Such a pretty stone, to pretty to be hidden.

I touched the chain, and pain seared into my mind. Not pain, power. Like my old strength but magnified, more. Channeled perfectly through the stone. I was still Yseult, a spaewife. But, for a time, at least, I could reach my magic.

Then the king took my other wrist. I lost hold of the stone and all my strength faded away.

I struggled a moment, and he slapped me, hard.

"You will obey me," he ordered, and my spine turned to water. If he wasn't holding my wrist, I would've collapsed.

A second later he thrust me onto the bed. I rolled to get away, and he caught my ankle, his fingers burning my skin.

I cried out. The ghosts rose up around the bed, faint hands reaching for me but unable to take hold.

The stone, the stone.

The king flipped me onto my back and slapped my

hands away. Catching the front of the gown, he tore neck to midriff.

Yes, the ghosts cried.

At my breast, the moonstone flared.

The king bellowed, throwing a hand over his face. I rose up, but a force tore the necklace from my throat and flung me away.

I fell as if from a great height. When I raised myself up, I was curled at the foot of the stairs in the throne room, weak and shivering. My chest bore bruises, my golden gown was rent down the front.

Gaul stood over me with a force of Berserker guards. "My liege, what orders do you have?"

"Take her away," the king ordered from his place high above on the dais. "Give her to the warriors for their satisfaction."

"My lord," Tristan marched forward, Ivar and Lars behind him. They saluted.

"A prize for you, commander," the king jerked his chin at me.

Ivar and Lars took my arms and towed me quickly out of the great hall.

"Steady," Lars whispered. Ahead, Magnus beckoned from the door.

Hope surged in me. They would take me from the castle. They would help me run.

We got so far as the outer courtyard, within sight of the yard, before a brace of warriors blocked our way.

Gaul stepped out, his weapon in hand. "She is our prize. She will be given to all of us."

A slick sound as Tristan drew his sword.

"Make way," he said.

None of the warriors moved.

"Make way," Tristan shouted, and the stones rang with his command, and the push of his authority. Sweat dripped down a few warrior's faces. Gaul gritted his teeth but did not budge.

Behind me, more weapons rang as they were unsheathed. Ivar, Lars, and Magnus would stand with their commander. Four against the rest. They would die.

"Wait," I rasped, and worked to clear my throat before repeating it, louder. When no one listened, I did the one thing I knew would bring their attention.

I stripped off the gown and let the moonlight wash over my bare form. Even bruised, my body tempted.

Amid the murmurs, I tossed the fine garment to the ground and stood naked before them.

"I yield," I told them. "Let it be as the king commands."

I walked past Tristan to the middle of the yard. By the time I reached the post that stood there, Magnus was at my side. Ivar and Lars joined us.

"Here," I grasped the rope hanging from the post.

"Forgive me, lady," Ivar murmured, and tied my hands above my head. I closed my eyes and waited for the Berserkers to come and claim me. I would be fodder for their lust and it would be the end. What remained of me at dawn would be given to the king for use as sacrifice.

A breeze caressed my face. I tilted my face up to the moon and prayed. *Goddess, let it be quick.*

I waited long moments, but nothing happened.

I opened my eyes... and saw nothing but Magnus' huge bulk before me. He stood poised, balanced on the balls of his feet, ready to fight. Ivar and Lars stood on either side of him, their swords out. Tristan stood by, too, his long cloak fluttering in the wind. The minutes crawled by and they did not leave my side. I had no powers, but I had four protectors.

Wind picked up and then the rain came, the Berserkers dispersed. Gaul led his away, muttering.

"Lady," Lars was at my side, untying me. As soon as my arms fell, I lurched forward, and was caught up in strong arms. Something soft and warm wrapped around my body. Red. Tristan's cloak

He carried me to the guard room where I'd eaten and set me on the table. He tsked as he examined my battered body and tucked the cloak tightly around me.

"What now?" I asked him, willing my teeth not to chatter.

"We will protect you. We will fight to get you free."

"The mage—I must—"

"We will fight to defeat him. No," he stopped my protest with fingers at my lips. "You cannot stop us. We will be your champions."

"Commander," Magnus said at the door. When he stepped back, I braced myself for Gaul to enter, but instead, a warrior came in and removed his helm. I did not recognize him, but he gazed at me as if I was the Goddess incarnate.

"What is it?" Tristan asked.

"Speak, man."

"Lady," the warrior said, and stopped.

Ivar came forward and put a hand on the warrior's back. "He wishes you to bless him."

I looked from Ivar to Magnus, but they said no more, so I beckoned the warrior forward.

He knelt before me and I laid a hand on his brow, like a mother would with a son. "I bless you." A whisper at my side and I knew his name. "Gavin. Remember your mother and the name she gave you."

"Lady," he murmured and rose, and another took his place. And another. The warriors crowded into the room, huge hulking men all clad in armor, bearing weapons. They knelt before me and I named them all, aided by the whispers.

At one point, Tristan paused the line to hand me a cup of water. "Thank you for telling me their names."

His brow furrowed but another warrior came in and knelt, and I did not have time to ask him why he looked confused.

My head bowed, my voice grew hoarse, but I blessed each man who came. A few did not appear—Gaul, and his followers.

Another lull, and Tristan handed me my cup. "That was the last."

"Not quite." Magnus strode from the door and sank to his knees. His head barely dipped below mine because of his great height.

I smiled and lay my hand on his brow. "I bless you—"

Magnus, someone at my right whispered. The voice did not belong to Tristan or Ivar or Lars. I turned in shock. A tall woman stood at my side, her features similar to the warrior at my feet. She seemed so solid, but a little movement of the candlelight and her essence shimmered. *Magnus,* the ghost repeated. *Son of Berta.*

I found my voice and repeated what the woman said.

Ivar son of Asta, a woman with dark, serious eyes came forward.

And Lars. A red-cheeked woman with blonde braids down her back smiled at her son. *Son of Hilde.*

Tristan son of Diana. The ghost of Tristan's mother stood tall and regal. Light flickered at her neck where the moon-stone would've rested.

Tears pricked my eyes as I gazed at the waiting faces.

The warriors ranged in front of me, and behind them, the ghosts of the king's wives, their mother's.

I'd come all this way to this time, I'd failed my mission, but at least I'd freed them.

"Lady," Tristan said. "We are yours. You have but to command."

No. I could not ask them to die. In the morning I'd face the Corpse King and let him deal with me as he would, even if he sacrificed me to his power.

But that was tomorrow. It was still not yet dawn.

"We have one night," I whispered. "I have only one wish. Not a command."

"Order us how you will."

It was only us, the ghosts had gone. I slipped off the table and let the cloak fall open. I stood before them, not a witch, not a maid, just myself. Yseult.

"What do you want?" Tristan asked.

"You," I said to him and the three men beyond. "All of you."

Reaching back, I undid my braid and shook it out so the white flowers fell around me. I was nervous as a virgin, and perhaps I was, for this would be the first time I'd bared my heart to a man.

"You would lay with us?" Magnus asked, his rough voice choked.

"All of you."

"You honor us." Tristan lay down his sword and undid his armor. I rose to help. His three brothers waited at his back.

"Come. I need you." I fell back and let my hair halo around me, pale as moonlight.

I shuddered as I lay out before them, and again as the

warriors clustered around to gaze on my prone form. Desire curled in my belly, coiled tight and ready to burst.

"Lady—" Tristan breathed.

"Just Yseult. Just myself."

"To us, you are everything."

Tristan moved first. His hand closed around my ankle, gentle, but possessive. He had a right to touch me.

His hand skimmed upward, and I trembled. My hands reached for him. He leaned close and I drew him down so he lay over me, propping his weight on his muscled arms.

When we sparred with wit and will, I forgot how much larger these men were than me. I was small and lithe compared to their hard-muscled bulk. He rested his large hand at my collarbone and slid it up to collar me. Blunt fingers played over my pulse, strong enough to snap my neck, but remaining gentle. His touch stoked the fire between my legs.

"Commander," I whispered, and his thumb touched my lips.

"Call me Tristan."

We were as close as we could be. Tristan nuzzled at my breast, breathing in my scent.

"Take me. I am yours."

My hands tugged at his shoulders until he took my wrists and pinned them on either side of my head. I arched under him, tilting my hips up, reveling in his strength.

"I am ready."

"Tristan," I sobbed, my hips rising dying for contact with him. "Tristan."

"Shhhhh, my lady." Gentle hands turned my face to the side so Tristan could dip his head along mine and breathe in my scent.

"Please," I whispered.

He touched me, his large hands stroking down my body, bringing it to life. I hooked my arms around his neck, tugged him closer, but he growled and pinned them again. He kissed down my body as I writhed in his hold.

Then they were all there—all four—kissing and claiming me, marking me for their own. Lips caressed my ankles, my shoulders, my breasts. Tristan sampled my mouth, swallowed my moans. Fingers found the dew at my center and stroked in lazy circles.

"Please," my body went taut as a bowstring under that insistent touch.

"Soon," Tristan murmured into my ear. "We will fill you soon enough."

A finger slid inside, withdrew. "Now," I panted.

"No, not until we are ready." And they proceeded to make me writhe. I was a woman, I was a goddess, and they worshipped me every way they knew how.

Finally, finally, they deemed me ready. Tristan was first to fill me. His great body worked over mine. I ran my nails down his back and hooked my calf over his massive thigh, feeling the iron band of muscle flex as he rocked in and out of me.

Pleasure rushed through me; I cried out and scored his back when he slowed his thrusts.

"No—don't stop."

He sped until the table shook under us. The storm caught me up again, sent me soaring. I came down, grounded under Tristan's sated body. The great warrior held himself over me, keeping our hips joined. Ivar and Lars stood on either side, fondling my breasts, watching my face.

Someone tugged my head backwards with fingers in my hair. Magnus. The giant warrior was naked at the head of the table. His bearded face descended, and his mouth claimed mine, surprisingly soft. I sighed against his lips as Tristan's body left mine.

Lars took his place and stroked my legs until I looked at him. "You're sure?"

I rolled and rose to hands and knees before backing towards him. He grasped my hips and pulled me flush to his hips. As his cock nudged into me, I ducked my head and took Magnus into my mouth. The large cock stretched my lips, barely fitting between them. I swirled my tongue over the head as Lars started to drive into my wet heat.

When it was Ivar's turn, they flipped me again. My head fell back so Magnus could dip his cock into my mouth, sliding it further in. Ivar propped my legs against his shoulders, folding me in half as he fucked me.

"Lady," he pulled me close. His mouth worked at my neck, sucking at one spot until I melted. His teeth pierced me, agony flashed through me, followed by ecstasy. I bucked in his arms. "Mine," the swarthy warrior growled.

"And mine," Lars pressed into me from behind, lifting my hair and marking my shoulder.

"Forever," Tristan kissed me as I leaned against him, drunk with pleasure. His teeth scraped my opposite shoulder before delivering the mating bite.

In this way, Berserkers claim their mates. The bond would grow between us, our lives entwined until my death, when they would follow me into the beyond.

"Oh no," I sobbed. "No." I did not want to give them back their lives, just to end them.

"Yes," Tristan said. "So marked. So mated."

Ivar and Lars echoed his words, the blond adding, "We wish to be with you."

"Always," Ivar nodded.

"Our lady," Magnus gathered me in his arms. For all his

great size, he was so gentle as he arranged me on his lap. The iron bar of his cock lay between us. Grasping my hips, he slid me against him, drawing on my desire until my body wept for him. With fingers in my hair, he tipped my head back and laved his tongue over my pulse—once, twice. The third time he bit and sent me screaming into the heights.

20

YSEULT

I woke wrapped in Tristan's cloak. I lay on the table, still in the guardroom, but alone. The lingering darkness told me it was not yet dawn.

As I sat up, the cloak fell away. My body shone pale in the darkness, all the marks and bruises healed. All except the tender spots at my neck where the Berserkers had marked me. I'd lost the moonstone necklace, but they made one of their own. Their bites collared my neck.

They'd left my shift and boots beside a cup of water and honeycake. I dressed and stretched slowly, filled with the delicious ache. My men had claimed me.

But now it was almost morning, and they were gone.

After one bite of the honeycake, I heard a sound beyond the heavy silence. Sounds of battle. Sounds of death.

No. I rushed to the door. Finding the yard empty, I ran to the open gate. Gathered in the pre-morning gloom beyond the castle, the practice field was full of Berserkers. They weren't sparring. They were fighting, some holding the line, others driving forward, roaring. I spotted Ivar's bearded face under his helm, and Lars' bright head. A dark figure stood in shining armor on a hill beyond, overseeing the battle to destroy those loyal to the Corpse King. Brother fought brother and the grass was red.

"Lady," Magnus bellowed from his place fighting near the wall. "Get back!"

I retreated, only to back into a knot of warriors.

"This is your fault," Gaul snarled, grasping my arm and tugging me into the castle.

"No," Magnus threw off his opponents and ran, but the gates slammed down, locking him out. Locking me in.

Cursing, Gaul dragged me along. I fought to keep my feet.

"Where are you taking me?"

"To the king." Instead of leading me into a hall, he pulled me to the stairs. The mage stood amid a storm cloud of magic, his hands blurring as he worked spells.

Oily power crawled over my skin, setting me shuddering.

Ghosts clustered in the shadows of the wall.

"Help me," I pleaded.

"There is no one to save you. The king has too much might. He will destroy his army and raise another, stronger, in its place."

Gaul thrust me onto the parapet.

The king spared me not a glance, but I heard his voice in my head. *Just in time. Watch your Berserkers die.*

The tide had turned on the field of battle. When one Berserker fell, a spirit rose up in its place—dark and grotesque, made of evil magic. Twice the size of Magnus, they smashed through the ranks of warriors, splintering shields.

"Hold," Tristan shouted on the hill, and his men formed a line, only to scatter when a ball of fire blasted from the wall.

Smoke rose and I cried out. Lars and Ivar were among those on the line thrown to the ground.

Above me the mage cackled. His feet rose from the wall as the magic carried him higher, but he remained fixed on his purpose: destroying his own soldiers.

Magnus roared, facing the monsters risen from the bodies of his former warrior brothers. The Corpse King was earning his name, raising the dead.

"Goddess," I moaned, clinging to the flagstones as the wind blew bitter ash over the wall. Fire spurted from the mage's hands again and again. I could fight the wind to reach him, but he could easily cast me down from the wall.

"Yseult," a voice on the wind. Tristan had left his post and was scaling the wall.

"No," I choked out. He risked his life for me, the brave, beautiful fool.

Gaul and his troops headed to the edge, as Tristan reached the top, they were waiting.

"No," I screamed as sword rang on sword. One of the warriors fell, tossed by Tristan over the wall. The rest rushed him as one.

The stone, a ghost whispered. Diana, Tristan's mother stood at my side. *Use the stone.*

I felt a weight in my sash. Sure enough, when I reached in I pulled out the moonstone Tristan had used to test me.

To my right the mage hovered over the wall, working his spells. He no longer looked a man, but an apparition, a misty form clad in lightning. To my left, Tristan thrust his sword through Gaul's chest and dropped him off the wall, then whirled to face the remaining Berserker's spears.

Now, more ghosts joined Diana.

Look to the horizon. It is time, Hilde said.

Daylight weakens him. Added Asta, even as the sun's first rays slanted through the fearsome figure of the mage. *He can be defeated. It will take all you have.* She nodded to my hands. *Use the stone.*

I clutched it and felt the rush of my powers, just beyond reach. I was still not a witch, still weak. Weak enough to penetrate the mage's defenses.

Strong enough to give my life for my men.

I had to save them.

"Help me," I told the ghosts, and, as Tristan snarled, pinned by spears, I raced towards the mage, leaping at the last. Ghostly hands carried me aloft. The air crackled with magic, my hair whipped about my face. But my arms were strong, steadied by the will of many, all the wives of the Corpse King, unwilling to watch their sons be victims of his rule.

"Lycaon," I shouted even as the mage's magic threatened to blast the skin from my bones. "I bind you." I thrust the stone into his heart.

Lightning blinded. Thunder cracked. Screams rent the air as the mage's power broke. The backlash threw me from the castle walls. Ghostly hands held me aloft for a few seconds, then a hard body hit mine and we fell.

When I woke, dazed, the Earth was being torn apart. The very foundations of the castle shook with the dismemberment of the Corpse King's power. The walls cracked, falling. Stones smashing to the ground, to dust.

But it was too late. All around me dead Berserkers lay, their blood seeping out, sealing the Corpse King's tomb.

Tristan stretched beneath me. He'd cushioned my fall, but now he lay still.

"No," I sobbed. "No." I'd bound the Corpse King, but at too high a price.

21

YSEULT

D awn broke. I heard my sisters chanting the echoes of the spell that sent me across time.

When shall we all meet again?

The words drowned out in the howling of the Corpse King's destruction.

But I heard them still, spoken by ghostly voices.

the spell we set is done,
the battle's lost and won...

"Tristan," I croaked, even though he lay still as death. I pulled myself over him and lay my head on his chest to listen for the beating of his heart. Around me, very faintly, I felt the tethers of the Berserker bond linking me to my men. All fallen. All dying.

With the rising of the sun...

With the last strength in me, I mouthed the verse and tugged on the Berserker bond. We would be together no matter what took us—the spell or death.

Magic ripped through my body, wrenching me apart. The air split. Howling wind filled my ears as a thousand years passed in a second.

Silence. Breath rushed back into my lungs. I lay on my back for a moment, stunned. Sensation returned, and I held back my groans. My body felt like it had been beaten.

Wind swept over my face, bringing with it the familiar stench. The spell was completed. I was home.

I sat up. The spell had brought me back to my own time. I recognized the ravaged plain. As desolate and rocky as I'd left it, but, here and there, a few white flowers bloomed.

There can be good in the world if flowers can still bloom.

Something flashed in the corner of my eye. I looked but there was nothing. A ghost?

Then I felt it, under the beating of my heart—the faint pulse of the mating bond. Four bonds, different, but equally strong.

I hastened to my feet, staggered in the direction of the ghostly messenger. My breath sawed through me as I prayed, stumbling over the lichen covered rocks in my haste.

Tristan lay in a bed of heather, his face still. I flung myself down. His chest rose and fell. Lars lay nearby on the right, Ivar on the left. Magnus' great bulk some yards away.

I had done it. I'd brought them to my time.

When I touched his face, Tristan opened his eyes. Blood and muck marred his face and body, but he was alive.

"Tristan," I whispered.

"Yseult? What happened?"

"We are here. At my home."

He started to rise and groaned. I lay a hand on him.

"Shhh, easy. Stay down for now. We are safe."

"What is that stench?"

"The Corpse King's tomb," I half laughed. "We sealed it in your time. It broke open again."

His eyes widened. "So we have come—"

"A thousand years from your time, love," I told him. Around us, the other men were stirring.

"Sister," a wavering voice called. "Yseult."

Tristan reached for his sword—which was gone—and I pressed him down again.

"It's only the witches. My sisters." If I could still call them that. My powers were still gone.

The coven hurried toward us, led by the most ancient one, who moved with a speed beyond her years. Behind her was Sabine, my student, with her mates at her side. As soon as they saw Tristan and three other strange warriors, they stepped forward with weapons drawn.

"Stop." I found myself on my feet. "These men are friends. They aided me."

"Then the spell worked? Did you find him?" Several witches spoke at once. Not the ancient one, who only studied me with beady eyes.

"I did. I faced the Corpse King, and survived, thanks to these men." Despite his wounds, Tristan rose at my side. Ivar and Lars helped each other up. "They helped me escape the mage's magic."

The ancient witch approached. Tristan started to insert himself between us and I stopped him. For a moment the crone only studied me, then nodded once. Satisfied, she turned and walked away.

"You have the spell?" Sabine asked.

I nodded and let myself lean on Tristan. My palms burned where I'd clutched the stone and thrust it into the

Corpse King's heart. The lore told of the spaewife who bound the mage for a thousand years, and now I knew the truth.

It was me.

"I have the spell," I let the wind carry my voice to all my sisters. "I know how to defeat him."

EPILOGUE
YSEULT

Over the years, I'd traveled far and wide, but a simple cave was my home. It was deep within the Earth, guarded by much magic.

I invited my sisters to journey there from the moor so we could speak in safety. I wished I could rest and hide away, like a creature weakened by a predator hides to heal. As if sensing this,

My warriors aligned themselves around me, a fearsome honor guard. I noted Sabine's mates did the same, though when their paths grew close to my four, they gave each other respectful nods. They did not, however, take their hands from their weapons.

When we came to my dwelling, I felt a rush of panic. I'd spent many years layering the wards, but now, with my magic stripped, would they recognize me?

"It's all right, child," The crone was suddenly at my side. She had disappeared on the walk—I had looked for her. Of all my sisters, I most wished to speak to her.

She nodded to the hillock that hid my cave's entrance. "Approach as you would."

Bidding my retinue wait, I continued on unsteady feet. A harsh second, and the ground yawned before me, a tunnel leading into the hill. As I stepped by to let the group pass, the crone hung back to tell me, "Well done, child."

I stiffened to hide my shaking. I did not feel my power as before, but it seemed to be there, lying still, but deep and vast, a somnolent sea.

"My lady," Tristan drew close and took my elbow.

"I am fine."

His tight smile told me he knew I was lying. A low order, and his captains took up the rear of the group, along with Sabine's mates.

"We will post a guard," he said, and shook his head before I could protest that my wards would hold. "One of us and one of them."

Frowning, I plucked at his filthy armor. My hand reached the skin underneath. It was warm and smooth. His wounds had healed. "Berserker magic," I muttered, though perhaps my sisters had quietly helped. I was glad of it, but I wished I could've been the one to heal them.

"We are fine, lady. Let us do our duty."

I sighed. I was not used to having protectors, but it seemed, now I did.

As my sisters filled my hall, Sabine headed to the hearth. Because of her training, she'd been here many times, and would know what to do to make all welcome. She directed a few novices to serve food and drink, starting with my warriors. I waved away everything until Tristan knelt at my side with a cup and would not take food himself until I drank.

My face and body remained composed, even as whispers floated around the room. My sisters wondered what had happened, why my visage was so changed, and why I had returned with mates.

I sipped from my cup, my other hand trembling under the robe Tristan placed on my shoulders. To all in my time, I was the powerful witch Yseult. The spell had brought me down to the level of a novice, but I would not show weakness. Not if I could help it.

The crone watched all of this from a corner, perched like a raven on a large barrel. Nothing escaped her beady black eyes.

Tristan remained close, almost pressed to my side, as if he sensed my distress. He was still in his armor, though he'd washed his face and hands, and cleaned away the traces of battle.

At last, I set the cup down and laced my fingers together. There, with my sisters ranged about the fire, I told the whole story.

"It is done," a novice breathed at the end.

"Not quite," an elder answered. "She bound him in that time. The spell lasted for a thousand years and has now worn off. We must face the mage again."

"You were the spaewife who first bound him?" another asked.

I nodded. "In that time, I had no magic. My spaewife abilities returned."

"Has your magic returned?" For a moment I hated the novice, even though she'd only asked what was on every one of my sister's minds.

"Returned?" cackled the crone. "Why should it return? It never left." Her black eyes fixed on me. "She is a spaewife, and a witch."

"Not quite," I said. "My powers are different."

"Changed. Not less." The crone slipped from her seat.

"Enough. We have much to do. We must find the moonstone and plan a way to approach the mage to cast the spell. Not you," she put a hand on Tristan's shoulder, and though he blinked in surprise, he allowed it. "You have done much. You must rest."

My sisters all rose, fluttering about like hens.

"Is there anything I can do for you?" Sabine asked, and I thanked her.

"We will return," her mates told Tristan. "We will be keeping watch of this place while you rest. In a few days, we wish you to join us on a hunt."

My mate agreed.

"Yseult," the crone called me, and though her voice was soft, I heard it sharply. "I wish to speak to you. Alone." She held up a hand when Tristan hovered at my shoulder. "I will not harm your lady. I give you my word, commander."

Tristan bowed. "I will speak to my men."

I watched him stride away, strong and powerful, even in my small home.

One by one the witches left. I waited until the last had gone, and then sank down to the hearth.

The crone prodded my hand with a cup. "Drink this."

I did and sucked in a breath at the rush of energy that followed.

"My own brew." She winked at me with her raven black eyes. "So, Yseult. You faced the mad king and saved your Berserkers, all without your powers."

"Not by choice." I met her gaze. "You knew all along?"

She shrugged. "The Corpse King would not allow a powerful witch to approach him. Only a maid, weak and lowly, could get close enough to destroy him."

"Then it was your intent all along. You wove the spell." I set the cup down. "Why didn't you warn me?"

"If I had, would you have gone? Given up your powers and gone on despite it?"

I pressed my lips together. I truly didn't know.

She cackled and patted my hand. "What's done is done. You did well, child."

"There is still a job to be done."

"And it will be done. You have shown us the way. You may well be the one to bind him again."

I nodded. "I must be ready. I must work to regain my power."

"You have power, child. You are a spaewife. You had it all along."

"I rejected that path when I became a witch."

"Yes, but the Goddess had another plan. You sought a way to make yourself strong, strong enough to fight a man and rule over him."

"That is not why I chose the path," I protested.

"It doesn't matter. You did not need the witch's path to do that. Perhaps you can have both." A smile stretched her ugly, wrinkled face.

A clink of swords, and I looked up as four large warriors strode in. The smell of roasted meat wafted with them. Magnus brought up the rear, still tearing at leg of meat.

My shoulders slumped. I had not even thought to feed them.

"They are men, not boys. They can hunt for themselves." The crone rose and faced Tristan. "We will want to examine you, later. See if there are any lingering effects of the spell. But first we will let you rest."

I followed the ancient witch to the mouth of my cave.

"Go to them. They are fed and rested, but still hungry for you." She gave me a slight push, when I looked back over my shoulder in the direction she left, I was alone.

I ambled back inside and stopped short as the giant warriors turned as one to me.

"Lady," Ivar said softly, and I realized I'd been staring at them. I had never brought a man into my home. Now I had four.

I cleared my throat. "There are pools deeper in the caves, if you wish to bathe."

"Do you wish us to bathe?" Ivar asked.

Lars slapped his shoulder. "She's trying to tell us we stink."

"Speak for yourself," Ivar shook off his hand. "I smell like a man."

"Perhaps she likes our scent, but simply wishes to strip us of our armor," joked Lars.

I flushed like a maid at their teasing.

"I know I stink," Magnus said. He ripped the last of the meat off the bone. I opened my mouth to tell him how to dispose of the bone, but he tossed it to the floor.

"You're a pig," Ivar told him.

Magnus shrugged.

"Enough," Tristan ordered. "Let us do as our lady bids."

"Wait," I cleared my throat. "I have to tell you something. I have never taken a man back into my quarters. My home, I mean. You are the first."

"We are the only men to come here?" Lars grinned.

"Yes." I blushed again. To everyone else, I was a powerful witch. To these men, I would always feel like a maid on the eve of becoming a woman.

Tristan moved first.

"We are honored, lady. What can we do to set you at ease? We are yours to command."

I smiled shakily. "You should bathe. And dress. I can find

clothes for this age. I can tell you many things of what has gone before this time, between my life and yours."

"A thousand years of history," Tristan said thoughtfully. "That will take many nights."

"Not how I'd choose to spend them," Lars grumbled.

"Oh, Goddess," I raised my hands to my face.

"What about you, Yseult?" Ivar asked.

I lowered my hands but kept them covering my bright cheeks. "Me?"

"We had one night, lady. We've known you a day. We wish to know more about you."

I sank into a chair.

"Enough. All of that can wait," Tristan said, and crouched down beside me. "You are tired, lady."

"A little. It's been a long day."

"We will rest," Tristan said.

"All of us?" Lars asked.

"All but one. The one will remain with our lady. Alone."

"I'm not tired," Magnus said.

"Alone?" Lars perked up.

"One at a time," Tristan repeated firmly.

"Is this acceptable, lady?" Ivar asked.

"Yes, that would be good." I said in a shaky rush of breath.

"Right. Then me first." Lars said, removing his helm.

"What?" Magnus said. "Why you?"

"Because I am the youngest. And of all of us, I have had the pleasure of making our lady laugh."

His bold proclamation brought an easy smile to my lips.

"He's right," Ivar said.

"Then it's settled," Tristan said. "Where will be our quarters?" I pointed to a storeroom and showed them the shelves of extra furs. We would have to find a larger sleeping chamber. Later. After I figured out how to live with four giant warrior men.

How would I feed them all? Where would we sleep?

"Thank you, lady," Tristan murmured.

"Thank you," Ivar and Magnus added, bowing to me. Tears pricked my eyes. I'd found these men to almost just lose them. Even now, we had dangers to face. Who knew what the future held.

"Don't cry, Yseult," Lars took my hand and kissed it, ever the charmer. "We have but one night, but after your time with my warrior brothers, I will return."

"You will not have her the whole night," Magnus growled. "I need little sleep."

"It will not take me a night to spoil her for all others."

Barking a laugh, Magnus went into the storeroom. I caught Ivar winking at me just before Tristan shut the door.

"Finally," Lars turned with a grin. He'd stripped off his armor and was tying back his hair. "It's only us."

"Yes."

"You're shaking." Frowning, he led me to the fire.

"It's not that." I rubbed my face. "I'm not cold."

"Lady, you have no need to fear us."

"I know that. I know. I just..."

He hushed me and pulled me down to the rug before the hearth, drawing a robe over us. "Sleep, lady. I will watch over you."

"You don't have to do this," I whispered. "I am used to guarding my back. I am used to being alone."

He spent some time stroking the hair from my face. "Perhaps you have been alone too long."

"I—"

But he stopped me with a kiss, gentle and chaste, and

turned me on my side before him, one strong arm pulling my back to his front. "Sleep now."

Mercifully, I did.

But then I dreamed. There the Corpse King chased me, his skeletal hands grasping. Round and round we went, as the Berserkers lay in a field of blood.

"Yseult, Yseult," someone shook me. I came awake with a cry.

The fire had burned down to embers. Ivar leaned over me, his face somber. He cradled my head and set a cup to my lips. After I drank, he drew me into his arms, and kept me there while I pressed my face to his neck and cried.

"Sweet Yseult," he stroked my back. "Tell me your dreams."

I shuddered. I hadn't cried so hard since my training as a novice. "I dreamed your deaths." I couldn't say more than that; it was too awful. Ivar nodded as if he knew.

"I wish to bathe. Will you show me how?"

At last, something I could do. Taking a torch, I led him through the cave to a special place I'd found where hot springs bubbled from the Earth.

"This is why I made my home here."

"You lived here alone?"

"Since I left the novices and made my own path as a witch."

"I see." He crouched and tested the water, then stripped off his clothes. I caught my breath at the rippling muscles of his back and swayed on my feet as he turned and came toward me. He didn't seem to notice my shock and desire. "I'm going to wash you now." He waited for me to nod, then helped me off with my shift and led me by the hand into the water.

There I stood shyly, head bowed, as he ran a cloth all over my body. He took his time.

"Ivar," I pressed myself against him.

Dipping his head, his mouth caught mine. My arms twined around his shoulders and we drank deeply of each other until someone cleared his throat nearby.

I stepped back, startled, to see Tristan waiting on the edge of the pool.

With a rueful grin, Ivar stepped back. "My time is over."

A sigh escaped me as the warrior strode away. Drops of water beaded on his bronze skin, rolling down his back to the dimples between his hips, down the cleft of his ass.

Tristan cleared his throat again. "Feeling better?"

"I am. I recommend a bath."

"Hmmm." He started stripping off his clothes. "The last time I bathed, I was interrupted."

"Such rudeness. I can't imagine."

"Yes, well, the sight of a pretty maid

"A maid?" I raised a brow. "Not a lady?"

"Both."

I pushed him away. "We have things to discuss."

"Oh?"

"Yes." I turned from him. "This morning I woke alone."

"Lady—"

"You left me in a guardroom!"

"It was not our intention. We planned to start the fight as a diversion and return to smuggle you to safety. Gaul was ready for us, and, in the heat of battle, we left you in the only place I thought you'd be safe. I knew our fight was futile. I hoped we might weaken the mage, so you could escape."

"You could've died. I didn't ask you to do that."

His arms came around me, "Yseult—"

"No," I tried to wrench away and could not. I clawed at his hold.

"I am sorry we left you. It was my decision, and mine alone."

"You took the decision from me." He treated me like I was weak.

His lips touched my ear. "How can I atone?"

"I don't know." My chest heaved against the pain squeezing my heart. "I don't know."

His lips touched my shoulder; he nuzzled my hair.

"I don't know if I can do this."

Gently he turned me to face him, but I couldn't meet his eyes. "I can't... be with you." I waved my hand in the direction of the cave.

"Be ours?"

"Be weak."

"Yseult." He lifted my wet hair away from my face. "You are not weak. You are not frail. You left your home. You faced the mage. Are you truly afraid of this?" He tipped up my chin. "Of us?"

"I don't... I should not fear anything. I haven't felt fear like this since my training as a novice."

He cocked his head, his large hand sliding under my hair to my nape.

"I am a witch no longer," I whispered. "Not in the way I was. I am..."

"Weak?"

"Powerless."

"To us you wield great power."

"You don't understand. All my life I trained to be a witch, and now I am one no longer. I am only a spaewife."

"Only?" His fingers flexed against my neck. "You came to

us, barefoot, clad only in a shift. You were our captive, and even then, you saved us."

"I am weak," I whispered.

"Strong enough to be our mate. Strong enough to love. If you are willing."

His fingers withdrew. He backed away, and I almost cried out and followed him. "We will not force this. We will let you think on it."

"Tristan," I called. He paused in the entrance. "Please... don't leave."

"We made our choice. We will wait for you to make yours."

I wish I could say I followed him right away, pulled him into my arms and pledged myself right there. The truth is, I took my time, pacing on the edge of the water, then standing still. My reflection had not changed. I still looked like a maid in the blush of youth. I could return to the witch's path, redo my training, become powerful again. Fight the mage, commune with my sisters and live... alone. Or I could remain a spaewife.

Or perhaps, I could do both. I had always walked my own path, and now, I had four men to help me.

A deep breath, and I willed myself to leave the pools. My shift clinging to my damp body, my feet bare, my wet hair stringing about my face, I padded back to the cave. Echoes of men's voices greeted me. They'd stoked up the fire and lounged around the hearth.

As soon as I stepped into the room, all eyes came to me, and I halted. Magnus sprawled on the rug, Ivar seated close to the fire, using a stick to poke some roast meat. Lars idly played with one of his braids. Tristan leaned on the hearth stone, his face half in shadow, half in light. All waiting, it seemed, for me.

Four men. Goddess, would I be enough?

Magnus moved first. "Lady," he breathed. I stood like a statue as he came forward and knelt before me. Mine to command, and me as nervous as a virgin, as a bride on her wedding night. Which was... laughable.

I was Yseult. Witch, spaewife, woman. No man made me nervous—unless I allowed it.

I smiled down at the great warrior. He returned my grin, and barely waited for me to shake back my hair before lifting the hem of my shift. He pressed his face against my belly, turning this way and that before sliding lower, breathing in my scent.

He lifted me easily, carrying me to the couch. I reached for him, but instead of falling between my legs and rutting, he parted my knees and licked my center. My body arched, my mouth falling open to be greeted by Lars' kiss. He and Ivar took turns claiming my mouth as Magnus worked below, their hands stroking my breasts until I cried out. The two on either side fell away as Magnus reared up over me, setting his cock into my sopping center, and slamming into me. I writhed in the throes of pleasure as he worked his hips, deep thrusts that sent me to the edge of ecstasy. When he was done he pulled out and Ivar and Lars took me together, hard and fast, one behind and one before. Lars cradled my chin as I licked at his cock.

They spent themselves together, and I lay over the edge of the couch, panting. Tristan still waited by the hearth.

Coming to my hands and knees, I crawled across the rug to him. Kneeling at his feet, I clutched his legs and tipped my head up, arching my back, and making my flesh an offering.

"Take me," I breathed. "I am yours to command."

He reached down and touched my cheek. I closed my

eyes and rubbed my face against his hand, my fingers busy parting his clothes. My fingers circled his thick cock, my mouth watering. I waited for him to press me forward then licked and sucked to my heart's content, my body aching to please him.

All too soon he cupped the back of my head and drew me up, kissing my forehead and hitching me against him and sliding home. I wrapped my legs tight around his hips, keeping him close as he moved inside me. His large hands gripped my bottom and I held him tight, my arms about his shoulders and my inner muscles gripping his cock. He was mine, I would keep him. I would never let him go.

He shuddered out his pleasure and laid me on the couch. I laughed, and kissed him, pulled Ivar close and kissed him too.

Lars joined me on the couch, nuzzling me.

"Keep us, Yseult," he mumbled. "We will make you so happy. We will protect and cherish you always. Do not send us away."

"Never," I whispered fiercely. "You are my heart." And I laughed and laughed as he kissed me with his ticklish blond beard.

Tristan came with a wet cloth and I grinned at him as he cleaned me.

"What now?" I asked, feeling rested and more refreshed than I had in an age.

"Whatever we want." Lars cupped my left breast and Ivar reached down from his perch on the arm of the couch to play with my right.

Magnus stood before me, staring at my bare form and absently tugging on his cock. His brow wrinkled.

"Wait," he said. "When is it my turn to have her alone?"

Read the next in the Berserker Brides series: Owned by the Berserkers starring Fern, Dagg & Svein
And Tamed by the Berserkers with Sorrel, Thorsteinn & Vik.

The Berserker Saga

Sold to the Berserkers - – Brenna, Samuel & Daegan
Mated to the Berserkers - – Brenna, Samuel & Daegan
Bred by the Berserkers (FREE novella only available at www.leesavino.com) - – Brenna, Samuel & Daegan
Taken by the Berserkers – Sabine, Ragnvald & Maddox
Given to the Berserkers – Muriel and her mates
Claimed by the Berserkers – Fleur and her mates

Berserker Brides

Rescued by the Berserker – Hazel & Knut
Captured by the Berserkers – Willow, Leif & Brokk
Kidnapped by the Berserkers – Sage, Thorbjorn & Rolf
Bonded to the Berserkers – Laurel, Haakon & Ulf
Berserker Babies – the sisters Brenna, Sabine, Muriel, Fleur and their mates
Night of the Berserkers – the witch Yseult's story
Owned by the Berserkers – Fern, Dagg & Svein
Tamed by the Berserkers — Sorrel, Thorsteinn & Vik
Mastered by the Berserkers - coming in 2020, Juliet and her mates

To my author friends – The Not RH authors Golden Angel, Aubrey Cara, Miranda Martin, Renee Rose, Ava Sinclair, Rebel West and Lili Zander. You earned your nipple tassels! Also to Miranda aka Mommy Is A Book Whore, for her fabulous last minute editing
And to the readers and fans in the Goddess Group, and everyone who bought this book. XOXO
Thanks for reading! –Lee

FREE BOOK

Get a secret Berserker book, Bred by the Berserkers (only to
the awesomesauce fans on Lee's email list)
Go here to get started... https://geni.us/BredBerserker

ALSO BY LEE SAVINO

Contemporary Romance

Her Marine Daddy

Her Dueling Daddies

Beauty & The Lumberjacks

Innocence: a dark mafia romance trilogy with Stasia Black

Beauty's Beast: a dark romance with Stasia Black

The Berserker Saga and Berserker Brides (menage werewolves)

Draekons (Dragons in Exile) with Lili Zander (menage alien dragons)

Bad Boy Alphas with Renee Rose (bad boy werewolves)

ABOUT THE AUTHOR

Lee Savino is a USA today bestselling author. She's also a mom and a choco-holic. She's written a bunch of books—all of them are "smexy" romance. Smexy, as in "smart and sexy."

She hopes you liked this book.

Find her at:
www.leesavino.com